LAST OF THE LONGHORNS

WILL ERMINE

SAGEBRUSH
Large Print Westerns

First published in Great Britain by Sampson Low
First published in the United States by Doubleday

First Isis Edition
published 2020
by arrangement with
Golden West Literary Agency

A catalogue record for this book is available
from the British Library.

ISBN 978–1–78541–696–5 (pb)

Published by
F. A. Thorpe (Publishing)
Anstey, Leicestershire

Set by Words & Graphics Ltd.
Anstey, Leicestershire
Printed and bound in Great Britain by
T. J. International Ltd., Padstow, Cornwall

This book is printed on acid-free paper

LAST OF THE LONGHORNS

For years, Morgan Cameron and Jim Brett have been working and planning for the day when Morgan's sons, Stash and Lee, will take over leadership of their combined empire, B C Company. Stash, who is determined to become sole boss by fair means or foul, finds his way continually blocked by his brother. But Lee, intent on keeping the peace, refuses to compromise where pretty Kit Mosby is concerned — and he vows that Stash will never have her, even if it means killing him to prevent it. When a cowardly murder rocks the range, even soft-spoken Jim gets his dander up. But that's only the beginning of gunsmoke and disaster. Violence soon breaks out in full force, and the powerful B C Company is divided into hostile factions, brother against brother, with vast cattle holdings and a woman's love at stake.

SPECIAL MESSAGE TO READERS

THE ULVERSCROFT FOUNDATION
(registered UK charity number 264873)
was established in 1972 to provide funds for
research, diagnosis and treatment of eye diseases.
Examples of major projects funded by
the Ulverscroft Foundation are:-

- The Children's Eye Unit at Moorfields Eye Hospital, London
- The Ulverscroft Children's Eye Unit at Great Ormond Street Hospital for Sick Children
- Funding research into eye diseases and treatment at the Department of Ophthalmology, University of Leicester
- The Ulverscroft Vision Research Group, Institute of Child Health
- Twin operating theatres at the Western Ophthalmic Hospital, London
- The Chair of Ophthalmology at the Royal Australian College of Ophthalmologists

You can help further the work of the Foundation
by making a donation or leaving a legacy.
Every contribution is gratefully received. If you
would like to help support the Foundation or
require further information, please contact:

THE ULVERSCROFT FOUNDATION
The Green, Bradgate Road, Anstey
Leicester LE7 7FU, England
Tel: (0116) 236 4325

website: www.foundation.ulverscroft.com

Contents

CHAPTER
ONE

Dirty Work at Grass Valley

Jim Brett's Light Buckboard, with its yellow wheels and running-gear, was a familiar sight in this section of Wyoming. Once a month he made the round of the Brett-Cameron Company's string of ranches. When snow made a rig impracticable he took to the saddle and went on, permitting nothing less than a blizzard to stop him.

He was no longer young, but for a quarter of a century and more he had looked the same, a thin, colorless man, always a little dusty-looking, who seldom found it necessary to raise his voice to have his orders carried out.

In his time Jim Brett had filled a hundred small leather-covered notebooks with memorandums concerning the needs and condition of the various ranches. It might be only a window at the Kelly Creek ranch that needed replacing, or the wastefulness of the cook at Deep Springs. In the latter case only the cook's name would be put down, with a question mark, which meant he was to be replaced. If a puncher gave evidence of loyalty to the brand and showed signs of being able to take charge of men, his name went into the book. The

Brett-Cameron Company often needed a foreman; when it did, someone was moved up from the ranks and the notations in Brett's little black book dictated the choice. Its judgments were so seldom wrong that it had long ago given rise to the saying that if a man was worth his salt he didn't have to move on to some other outfit to get his chance.

Brett was at the Grass Valley ranch this afternoon. It was the Brett-Cameron Company's home ranch, the acorn from which its empire of grass and cattle had grown. Here, in the long ago, Brett and his partner Morgan Cameron had come to rest with the hundred-odd longhorns they had driven all the way from Texas, looking for range that they intended to make their own by the simple process of having seen it first.

It was early in May now, and the calf branding had been going on for several days. Having inspected the house and other buildings inside and out and checked the supplies the cook had on hand, Jim sat on a bench under the big cottonwood near the kitchen door, busy with pencil and his current black book. Sitting there, waiting for the crew and Stash Cameron, Grass Valley's foreman, to come in, he had but to lift his eyes to see the pass through which he and Stash's father had crossed the Big Medicine Mountains and taken their first moments of mellow retrospection. Today was no exception.

If the familiar scene quickened old memories in him more sharply than usual this evening it was only because his musing had a gloomy twinge. He'd always had a great eye for locating trouble at a distance. For

2

the past several months he had been aware of the cloud on the horizon. It was still no bigger than the proverbial man's hand; but it was there, and it was growing.

No matter what comes, I'll never trade or sell my half interest in Grass Valley, he mused.

The thought shocked him, and he sat up a little stiffly and put away his notebook.

Morgan and I don't see things eye to eye any more, he admitted, *but it's unthinkable that we'd come to the parting of the ways after all these years.*

He shook his head over it and tried unsuccessfully to dismiss it from his mind. It might be unthinkable, but he knew stranger things happened every day. The trail Morgan Cameron and he had traveled had often been a rocky one, and they had had many differences, but they had always been able to work things out. Left to themselves, they could do it now.

Brett knew it was a vain hope.

It's Stash — he's driving a wedge between us — taking us in a direction I won't go.

He saw the crew coming in. His eyes were still keen, and he had no difficulty picking out Stash, tall in the saddle and square-shouldered. With his raven-black hair and gray eyes, he was a recognizable facsimile of the man his father had been at thirty-two.

The men began turning their broncs into the horse corral a few minutes later. Stash saw Brett and raised a hand in greeting before he got down. He could have turned his mount over to one of his punchers, but he snaked off his own saddle and bridle and gave the horse a slap on the rump.

Instead of going through the gate, the animal started to back off. Stash was instantly angered and gave the horse a kick that wrung a snort of pain from it. He would have repeated the performance if the bronc had not dashed into the corral.

It was a trivial thing but characteristic of Stash Cameron, Brett thought. He had fired men for less.

Stash sat down on the bench with him.

"When did you get in, Jim?"

"In the early afternoon. How are things going?"

"Okay. We'll finish up the branding tomorrow. The stuff looks good; fewer heifers than usual this spring."

They talked for half an hour about the condition of the ranch and stock.

"Have you seen Lafoon?" Stash asked.

Brett shook his head. "Not recently," he said. "I talked to him in town about two weeks ago. He won't sell."

"The hell he won't!" Stash ripped out. "I'll change his mind for him. Ben Lafoon has been stalling us off for a year and a half. I've had about enough of it; we need that range."

"We could use it," Brett agreed. "But we can't run him out."

Stash laughed unpleasantly. "You're getting soft, Jim. In the old days, when the Brett-Cameron outfit wanted something, they took it — one way or another."

Brett nodded. "I know. Times have changed. Ben's all right; he supported us when we had that sheep trouble around Ruby Lake."

4

"Sure!" Stash scoffed. "He knew that was the side of the bread his butter was on; he didn't want to see sheep come in any more than we did."

"No matter; I don't propose to have any run-in with him," Brett insisted. "And I don't want you to have any, Stash," he added, not raising his voice but giving his words a pointedness that young Cameron could not fail to understand. "You leave Ben to your father and me; we'll work out a deal with him."

It was a reprimand. Stash pretended to shrug it off.

"I know how the old man feels about it," he boasted. As one of the heirs presumptive to the Cameron half of the company, he was fed up with being told where to head in. "He's got a bellyful of Ben Lafoon, too. I know what I'm talking about."

Brett didn't miss the threat Stash was conveying. He took it in stride, and said quietly, "Your father and I will have a talk when I get back to Powder City." That was all he had any intention of saying about it. He got to his feet. "I better eat supper; I'm going on to Kelly Creek tonight."

They were halfway to the house when Stash squinted his eyes at a rider, still some distance away, who was pushing his bronc over the Grass Valley road at a determined lope.

"Someone from town," he muttered. "Looks like Old Stony . . . It's Stony, sure enough!"

A vague anxiety was in his tone. Stony Jackman, whose years of service with the Brett-Cameron Company went back almost to the beginning, had for

5

the last decade been Morgan Cameron's handy man, and only the most urgent errand ever took him away from Morgan's side.

"I hope it doesn't mean someone's sick," Jim Brett observed, sharing Stash's concern.

They stood there, waiting. Stony rode into the yard, a shriveled little man with a leathery-looking skin that had the color of old saddle leather. He had a note for Brett, but though he addressed himself to Stash he had no greeting for him.

"Yore pa says yo're to head for town right away," he announced. "He wants you there 'fore daylight."

"Why is he hustling me in like that?" Stash demanded. "What's gone wrong?"

"Nothin'." Old Stony always spared words when he had a message to deliver. "Yore brother's gittin' in from the East on Number 12. She's due at four-ten if she's on time. Morgan says yo're to be at the house in time for the two of yuh to go down to the depot to meet the kid."

"I'll be damned!" Stash whipped out explosively. "Lee can be gone for two years or more, and when he comes home he's got to show up at four in the morning! Didn't he write the old man he was coming?"

"Telegraphed," Stony responded laconically.

"It's a hell of a note," Stash growled. "I ain't finished with the branding; I been in the saddle since sunup; and now I'm to ride fifty miles tonight so I can be on hand to tell that young pup I'm glad he's back. The old man thinks if he snaps his fingers I got to jump. Who does he think he is, anyhow?"

6

Stony had no comment to make; he had delivered his message and that ended matters as far as he was concerned. Stash could rant and curse all he pleased, but he would be in town by daylight; when Morgan Cameron gave an order he was in the habit of being obeyed.

Without a further word Stony led his horse down to the corral; he had been told to stay the night at Grass Valley.

Stash's glance followed him, his eyes angry and defiant. He turned to Brett then, not hoping to enlist his support but determined to vent his spleen on someone.

"I'm surprised the old man didn't ask you to come in to join the welcome-home committee," he said thinly. "Lee would never have gone East to school if you hadn't put the bug in the old man's ear; he'd have stayed on one of the ranches like I've done, and done a little sweating. If you ask me, he's had it pretty damn' easy. But he ain't coming back to push me around."

"Lee will have changed considerably if he tries anything of the sort," Jim remarked. "It was never his way to push anyone around. He may be a few years younger than you, Stash, but he isn't a boy any more; that's something you want to remember. Don't set yourself against him till you have some reason."

"I ain't setting myself against him," Stash snapped. "But he don't want to pull any airs on me. I've read his letters, talking big about what he's going to do. A veterinarian — a glorified vet, that's all he is!"

7

"He's coming back to us with a lot more than that," Brett said precisely. "We lose five times as much stock to disease as we do to rustling and predatory animals. If Lee can show us how to lick blackleg and tick fever he'll be a very valuable man for the company." He glanced at his watch. "It's a long ride you've got, but not a hard one. You better have supper before you go."

Like Stony, he knew Stash would go to town. His sureness communicated itself to Stash and further infuriated the big man.

"To hell with eating!" he growled. "I'll shave and have a cup of coffee."

The crew was at the table when he stamped into the house. He ordered a horse caught and saddled and went on upstairs to his room.

The Grass Valley house was a barren roost these days, not a shade or curtain at any window and the furniture limited to table, chairs, and bunks.

Brett sat down with the men. It struck him that his presence produced a conscious restraint in the room. It was strange, for though he was the half owner of the big B C brand — long since dubbed "Before Christ" by some unknown cowboy wit — he prided himself on being close to his men, mindful of their welfare and always easy to approach.

Old Stony came in and took a seat beside Jim. He was friendly, but he was a Cameron man and he had no confidences to exchange with Morgan's partner. The latter expected none. He noticed, however, that the usual chaff that greeted Stony whenever the old puncher chanced to appear at one of the ranches was

8

missing this evening. It quickened his suspicion that, under cover, something was amiss, and now that he was looking for it he caught a definite tension in the air.

It puzzled and intrigued Brett. He knew it had nothing to do with Stash's going to town. His gaze wandered about the room but failed to reward him with any hint of what was wrong. The men were hungry and they ate heartily, seldom glancing up from their plates.

There was a clatter on the stairs. Stash Cameron hurried in. He wolfed down a piece of beef and swallowed a cup of black coffee. His eyes settled on Duke Rucker.

"Duke, you ramrod this outfit till I get back. I won't be gone more'n a day or two."

Duke nodded. They exchanged a glance that seemed to hold a secret understanding. Stash stormed out, banging the door behind him. In another minute he was riding away.

With his going the silence deepened. There wasn't any talk at all in the room, only the scraping of knives and forks and the rattling of dishes.

Brett, never a heavy eater, lingered over his coffee, wondering what to make of it. He had been anxious to get started for Kelly Creek. Suddenly he was in no hurry to leave.

Rucker was the first to get up, his supper finished. He started for the door, but he had taken only a step when it was flung open. Ben Lafoon stood there, a gun in his hand, facing the roomful of B C riders. He was a thin, wiry man. His eyes were deep in their sockets, and they glittered with a cold fury.

"Set down!" he barked at Rucker. "Keep your hands on the table, all of yuh!"

The crew froze at attention, and Lafoon advanced a step or two.

"Where's Stash Cameron?" he demanded, the fury that was riding him roughening his voice.

Ben Lafoon had killed two men in a blazing gun duel in the main street of Powder City some years back, but by Wyoming standards he was a peaceable man, prosperous and widely respected. There wasn't anything peaceable about him this evening.

His question went unanswered for a moment, the crew leaving it to Brett to do the talking.

Jim got to his feet. "Stash left here about fifteen minutes ago," he said in his quiet way. "He was called to town. I don't know why you're busting in here like this, Ben, with a gun in your fist."

Surprise touched Lafoon's rocky face at finding Jim Brett present. "So you're here," he growled. "That makes things a little clearer. I thought this business was some of young Cameron's dirty work. I'm damned if it don't set me back to find you mixed up in anythin' as rotten as this, Jim. I wouldn't put anythin' past Morg Cameron or that rat-eyed son of his, but I always figured you were a square shooter. Stands to reason, I reckon, that some of the Cameron dirt would rub off on you sooner or later."

Brett's mouth tightened under this verbal whiplashing, but he refused to lose his temper. "I still don't know what you're talking about, Ben."

10

"The hell you don't! B C wants my ranch. I been warned that I'd have my mind changed for me about not sellin'. You're puttin' the heat on me now. This business this afternoon was the first step. Just as sure as you're standin' there, you know some of this crew came through my fence, vented the brand on half a dozen cows, and topped it off by burnin' a skull and crossbones on 'em with a runnin' iron! This outfit can't make a laughin' stock out of me!"

The thing Brett had felt, the air of restraint and the feeling that something was being kept back from him, was fully explained now. Today wasn't the first time he had warned Stash against stepping on Lafoon's toes. Obviously Stash had flouted his authority and, either on his own or with the approval of his father, had staged this raid. He hadn't found it necessary to pick out a man or two and use any secrecy; the whole crew had been in on it. Brett kept his head; he realized his quarrel was not with the men.

"This was done without my knowledge, Ben," he said, his voice crisp and charged with feeling. "If I had known about it in time, it wouldn't have happened. I've told Stash three or four times that he wasn't to get into trouble with you. I didn't see anything of him until he came in this evening."

"But you got him headed for town in a hurry, didn't you? You knew I'd be here."

"No, Ben. His brother Lee is coming home. Morgan sent Stony out with word for Stash to come in at once."

Enraged as he was, Lafoon knew he had heard the truth. "More of the Cameron litter comin' home to be turned loose on me, eh?" he ripped out scathingly.

"Not if I have anything to say about it," said Brett. "You destroy those cows, Ben, and send me the bill."

"Oh, no, I won't send you any bill! I'll do better than that! I'll kill the next Brett-Cameron man I catch inside my line!" His blazing eyes swept the room and came to rest on Duke Rucker, Stash's straw boss. "I'll be watchin' for you!"

He'd had his say. Covering the crew with his gun, he backed out through the open door. A few seconds later he could be heard riding away. A clatter of hoofs accompanied him, proving he had not come alone.

The crew threw off its trance. Heads came around and faces were turned to Brett. He didn't try to hide his annoyance. He made them feel it, but he delivered no angry blast.

"I'm not going to ask who went through Lafoon's fence," he said. "It doesn't matter; you had your orders. I expect an order — good or bad — to be carried out." He turned to Duke Rucker. "You have my team harnessed and send a man to Kelly Creek with word that I won't be there till later in the week. I'm going to town."

CHAPTER
TWO

Trouble in Big Letters

It was often said that in the wide sweep of Wyoming lying between the Big Medicines and the Tetons, and particularly in Powder City itself, little happened in the affairs of men on which Morgan Cameron didn't sit in judgment, sooner or later.

It came close to being the truth. He owned the Powder City bank. If you wanted to borrow money, you saw Morg Cameron. If you wanted to run for public office, you saw him. Town marshal, sheriff, and county prosecutor were hand-picked by him. It enabled him always to have the law behind him, which not only gave whatever he was doing an air of legality but provided him with the unofficial authority to have things run his way. In several instances men who had incurred his enmity left town hurriedly without attempting to stand on their rights.

But Powder City had little reason to complain, for it was the apple of Morgan Cameron's eye. It was prosperous, and he had made it so. It had a good hotel that he had built, and the Cameron Hospital. There was not another within a hundred and fifty miles. If the town was a little wild, it was because he thought that was the way a cow town should be. Out on the range there was the big Brett-Cameron Company, spread all over the county, to guarantee Powder City's continuing prosperity.

It was wide of the mark to say, as some did, that Jim Brett made the snowballs and Morgan Cameron only tossed them. Brett had become the stockman of the two. He kept the ranches ticking; Morgan Cameron handled the financial end of the business.

It was an arrangement that had always been satisfactory to the partners, and at sixty Morg, gray as an eagle and putting on flesh around the middle but in many ways still the same rough, hard-hitting individual he had been when he came in from the range to set himself up as Powder City's leading citizen, saw no reason why the arrangement shouldn't continue indefinitely.

Always a light sleeper, he heard a horseman turn into the driveway that led past the house. He lit a match and glanced at the bedroom clock. It was a little after half-past three. He didn't bother to look out to see who the rider was. Pulling on his clothes in the dark, he went down the hall to his wife's door and rapped on it softly. Mattie was the one person in the world with whom he had schooled himself to be gentle.

"Stash just rode in," he told her. "Don't bother to get up, Mattie. We'll make some coffee and get the survey out and go down to the depot. The train's very likely to be late. You take your time about getting dressed."

14

"I've been awake for an hour, Morgan," Mrs. Cameron told him. "I'll be down before you and Eustace leave."

When young Lee was just a toddler and found Eustace difficult to say, he had shortened it to Stash. The nickname had stuck, but Mattie Cameron made it a rule never to use it.

"I ought to go down to the depot with you to meet Lee," she said.

Morg shook his head. "You been feeling too poorly, Mattie. The boy wouldn't want you to overdo yourself."

He went down the stairs of the big house. It was the best house in town, but he could have afforded a much better one. It was comfortable, and that was all he asked. A woman came in to do most of the work for Mattie. If he had had it his way she would have hired a second girl so that she wouldn't have had to lift a hand. He never indulged himself in luxury or extravagance. The loose spending of money was something he abhorred, and he often said that nobody was going to follow him around by the dollars he threw away. Nothing enraged him more than to have Stash come to town and squander two or three hundred dollars in a riotous night in the saloons and houses under the hill in the section of Powder City that faced the river. Stash's morals didn't interest him, but he resented having a son of his make what he called "a fool of himself."

He found Stash in the kitchen. The long ride had not mellowed the younger Cameron's temper. "It's a fine note, pulling me all the way in tonight!" he growled. "You know I'm busy with the calf branding. Lee could have come out to the ranch when he got ready if he wanted to see me."

"Your mother's ailing again," Morgan snapped. "She can't go down to the depot. She figured you should be here, and so did I." That ended the matter as far as he was concerned. "We've got time to make some coffee and fry a little bacon. You hungry?"

Stash nodded. "What's the matter with Ma?"

"Wilkins doesn't seem to know. If she doesn't pick up soon, he wants me to take her down to Denver to a specialist. I'll do whatever Doc says." He changed the subject abruptly. "Jim showed up at Grass Valley yet?"

"Yeah, he got in yesterday afternoon. He was going on to Kelly Creek last evening. He didn't have anything particular on his mind." Stash was at some pains to make it sound casual; he wanted to avoid being questioned about things at the ranch. "When I passed the observation station," he ran on, "I noticed there wasn't any horses in the corral. The Mosbys haven't closed up the place, have they?"

"No, they're just away. Been gone about ten days. They expected to be back before this. They may be on the same train with Lee."

Morgan filled the coffeepot and opened the stove. He found the bacon, and broke half a dozen eggs in a frying pan. Without bothering to glance at Stash, he said, "You been stopping at the station every time you pass and showing the Mosby girl a lot of attention. I hope your intentions ain't serious."

"What do you mean, serious?" Stash demanded, quick to pick him up.

16

"You know what I mean," was the blunt response. "The Mosbys are fine people, and she's a nice, sensible young woman and too damn' good for you, Stash. She could never go in double harness with you. You'd break her heart and kill her spirit in six months."

It straightened Stash up. "That's what you think," he retorted, with a thin, contemptuous laugh. "Coming from you, I suppose I got to take it."

"I don't care whether you do or not." Morgan's tone was flat and uncompromising. "It don't set easy on me to have to say anything of the sort to you, but the kind of women you associate with will never fit you to be the husband of a decent, upstanding girl like Kit Mosby."

"It ain't up to you to tell me off every time I turn around!" Stash whipped out hotly. "I'm old enough to know what I'm doing!"

"I doubt it sometimes. You're carrying my name around, and I got something to say about what you *do* with it. A man's entitled to a little fun, but you don't have to go hog-wild like you did the last time you was in. Blow your nose in this town and I hear about it sooner or later. Thank God your mother doesn't . . . I guess we can eat."

Stash kept his tongue, figuring that was the quickest and best way out. He knew his father had a friendly interest and deep respect for Professor Mosby and his daughter, looking up to them as a cut above himself and the run of folk in and around Powder City. Never before, however, had he expressed his regard so forcefully. The Mosbys were Virginians, as he was, and that had been enough to prejudice Morgan Cameron in their favor from the day they arrived in Powder City. But the bond was stronger than that; during the War Between the States he had ridden with Colonel John Mosby's rangers from the summer of 1863 to the final capitulation, twelve days after Lee's surrender at Appomattox.

All this was of little consequence to Stash except as it furthered his own cause. Kit Mosby had captured his fancy at first sight, and though he made little progress with her he was determined to have her for his own. He dismissed Justin Mosby, Kit's father, as just an amiable old dreamer, so wrapped up in his stars and planets that Kit was the real head of the family.

The little white building that stood on the Painted Meadows — the land the gift of Morgan Cameron — always referred to as an observatory by Professor Mosby, was unfailingly called the observation station, or just the station, by all rangemen and townspeople. Powder City had never come face to face with an astronomer until the professor arrived the previous summer and announced he had come to Wyoming to establish a small field observatory under the auspices of the Fleischmann Foundation, of New York City. The cowboy population knew nothing about the Fleischmann Foundation, though they admitted it sounded important, but it was their opinion that anyone who could get paid for sitting up half the night, looking into a telescope, was fooling somebody. However, important-looking gentlemen had arrived in Powder City from time to time and had themselves driven out to Painted Meadows and the station. It put a damper on the levity leveled, at the professor, and when Kit Mosby appeared at the dances at the Painted Meadows and Deep Creek schoolhouses her charm and graciousness brought a quick, complete surrender.

Stash and old Morg were at the kitchen table, eating in grumpy silence, when Mrs. Cameron came in. Though barely three weeks had passed since Stash had seen his mother last, he was struck by the change in her. She was thinner, and there were signs of suffering about her mouth. Her eyes still had their patient, unfailing kindness.

"I hear you ain't feeling well, Ma."

"No, but it's nothing serious. We've had such a cold spring. I'll be all right, now that the days are getting pleasant." Mattie had little reason for her optimism, but all her life she had made light of her problems.

She bent down and brushed Stash's cheek with her lips. This big son of hers had been a cruel disappointment to Mattie Cameron. He had been growing away from her for years, getting coarse and hard, and no one knew it better than she. Contrary to what Morgan believed, she wasn't ignorant of Stash's escapades. It was a streak in him that she couldn't understand.

"It was nice of you to come in, Eustace," she said. "I know Lee will appreciate it. I'd always planned to have a big party for him when he came home. I never dreamed I wouldn't even be able to go to the train to meet him. You don't mind having your father call you in?"

"It caught me at a bad time. But it's all right, Ma," Stash had the grace to add. "I'll hitch up the surrey and we can get started."

The train was only a few minutes late. From the depot platform Powder City spread out stark and ugly in the unflattering early morning light. Beyond town a fringe of willows marked the uncertain course of the Yellowhorse River, already shrunk to half its turbulent spring flood.

Stash sat in the surrey beside his father, busy with his thoughts, a sullen scowl on his face. Even as a boy he had never got along with his brother. Making no allowance for the fact that the youngster was the baby in the family and entitled to the favors he himself had once enjoyed had poisoned Stash against him. Once, while the family was still living at the Grass Valley ranch, a calico pony had been given to Lee. Jealous and resentful, Stash had stolen out on the range with a small-caliber rifle and waited for Lee to ride by. His shot had tumbled the boy from the saddle, and only Doc Wilkins's skill had pulled him through.

Though Morgan and Mattie Cameron had not referred to the incident in years, Stash knew they had not forgotten it. He was doubly sure that Lee hadn't. Countless other differences stood between them. Waiting for the train this morning, Stash told himself that if the old arguments didn't pop up again, new ones would arise to take their place. He wanted no part of it. His mind was set on making himself boss of the Brett-Cameron Company, and he didn't intend to have Lee getting in his way. It prompted a question.

"What's Lee going to do — sit around and take things easy?"

Morgan liked neither the question nor the insolent tone in which it was put. "Suppose you leave that to me," he retorted, bristling. "He'll hold up his end, same as I expect you to do! I suppose it would be asking too damned much of you to try to pull together with him. You started off wrong with Lee, and you've been wrong ever since. I ain't forgotten nothing that's happened. If I don't say any more it's because I promised your mother I wouldn't. But I'm warning you, Stash, don't you get too big for your britches with me. I know you been doing it with Jim."

"Is that what he says?"

"It's what I say! You can buckle down to a job and you know how to drive a bunch of men, but you just can't stand being told what to do. I've sided with you against Jim every time there's been an argument, and it's made a lot of bad feelings between him and me. He realizes I been standing up for you even though I knew you was dead wrong, like last fall when that early blizzard caught you with all that stuff up around the Sunlight Peaks. He warned you to get the stock down in time, but you wouldn't listen, so we lost about a hundred head."

"That's his story," Stash declared with biting sarcasm. "He's out to make me look bad with you. I've told you a dozen times, if he said anything to me about moving the stuff, I never heard it. If you had your eyes open, you'd see what he's leading up to." It was part of his plan to turn the old partners against each other. He had already succeeded in antagonizing Brett. If he could get rid of him, Stash felt he could get around his father.

"Jim knows you don't want to give up the bank and go back on the range," he continued. "If he can make me look like a bush — well, chances are you'll be ready to sell out to him. That's what Brett wants. He's had everything his own way for years. If you ask me, it's about time you showed him you got something to say about how things are run."

"Poppycock!" Morgan snorted. "Jim Brett's a square shooter."

But the thought lingered and began to build up in him. Maybe it was true that he had been so busy in other directions he had lost his grip on the Brett-Cameron Company. Even to consider this as a possibility was enough to plunge him into a glowering, tight-lipped silence as he searched his mind for something that would either confirm or refute it.

Stash said no more; he was satisfied that the seed he had dropped had fallen on fertile soil and would flower sooner if left to itself.

They heard Number 12 blowing for Powder City. It pulled Morgan out of his festering abstraction. He got down from the surrey and with Stash at his side walked the length of the platform and beyond, where there was a gravel path beside the tracks. The Pullmans never got as far as the platform; Number 12 was always a long train, stopping only to discharge passengers from Cheyenne and the East.

The train ground to a stop. Lee swung down the steps without waiting for the porter to put his box in place, and stood waving to them.

"That's him!" Morgan cried, pride in his voice as he hurried to greet the grinning, good-looking homecomer. They pumped hands heartily. "By grab, you look fine, Lee! You've grown. You're almost as tall as Stash."

"Not quite, I guess," said the young man. "It's great to be back. Everything looks about the same. You look good, Dad." He shook hands with his brother. "I hear you're the big boss at Grass Valley. Why didn't you ever write a fellow?"

"You know how it goes. You intend to, but you keep putting it off. I been busy, too."

"I bet you have. I'll pitch in and give you a hand. Didn't Mother come down with you?"

Morgan shook his head and told him why. "She's waiting for you at home. She'll be awful glad to see you, Lee. Stash, you grab one of his bags; I'll tote the other."

Two cars ahead the porter had put his box down and was assisting a young woman and a small, rotund man to alight. Stash was quick to see them.

"It's the Mosbys!" he exclaimed, his pleasure evident. "I'll give them a hand; the two of you can make out all right by yourselves." He was off at once without bothering to glance at his father.

"Go ahead," Morgan grumbled. He didn't object to the proffered courtesy to the Mosbys, but it annoyed him to have Stash take it on himself and leave Lee and him standing there. "You ask them to wait up a minute when they reach the platform," he called to Stash. "I want to make them acquainted with your brother."

Lee Cameron hadn't taken his attention off the young woman who had stepped down from the train. He not only envied Stash the privilege of assisting her with her luggage, but he was sure she would disappear if he blinked his eyes and he would wake up and find he had been dreaming, for since leaving Chicago he had seen Kit Mosby in the dining-car at every meal, timing himself so that he would be sure to find her there. On several occasions her eyes had strayed in his direction and been quickly pulled away. Blue eyes that were unforgettable. He was surprised and delighted to learn that Powder City was her destination and, better still, that his father and Stash were on such friendly terms with Dr. Mosby and her.

"They're Virginians," Morgan observed, "and real quality folks. It's a pleasure to have them with us." Briefly he told Lee who they were and why they were in Wyoming. "I reckon Justin Mosby is a big man in his field."

"He certainly is," Lee agreed. "He's lectured at Cornell several times. I can't imagine a girl like that roughing it out on the Painted Meadows."

Morgan laughed. "Those fine duds are for going-away purposes. Don't let 'em fool you, Lee; when she gets into a pair of overalls she really takes a man's eye."

Stash took care of the introductions.

"This is quite a surprise, Mr. Cameron," Kit told Lee. "I saw you in the diner every day. I never dreamed

24

you were bound for Powder City. I've heard your mother and father speak of you so often."

"It's too bad I wasn't wearing an identification tag," said Lee. He was flattered to have her acknowledge that she had noticed him. The morning wind stirred through her chestnut-colored hair. He couldn't help thinking it formed a perfect frame for her sensitive, intelligent face. Her smile was slow and engaging and gave him the feeling that he had her complete attention.

"You greatly favor your mother, young man," the professor remarked, and turning to Morgan he said, "I don't see much of you in him, Mr. Cameron, unless it's his size."

"No, he takes after his mother. Stash is cut more to my pattern." Morgan's tone betrayed no note of regret that this was so, but he secretly wished it were otherwise. He couldn't help noticing how much at ease Lee was with the Mosbys. The boy had an air of gentility and good breeding about him that Stash had never possessed. *Maybe one gentleman in the family is all I'm entitled to,* he thought. *I'm a pretty rough article myself.*

In the few minutes they stood there Stash was jealously aware of how well Kit and his younger brother got on together. He was glad when the chance meeting was over; the rankling thought that Lee had put him completely in the shade inflamed him.

"Whenever you find yourself on the Painted Meadows, Mr. Cameron," Kit called to Lee, "I hope you'll stop in."

25

"I sure will," he promised. He liked her use of the Wyoming idiom "stop in" instead of "drop in." Evidently she liked Wyoming and this western country and didn't consider herself too good for it.

Stash walked across the street to the hotel with the Mosbys. Morgan drove by a few moments later and picked him up.

"You sit back with Lee, Pa," Stash said. "I'll drive home."

It was never difficult for him to whip himself into an ugly mood. He was close to it now. He damned the chance in a thousand that had placed Lee on the same train with the Mosbys. *The young squirt!* he thought. *I'll put him in his place if he tries to cut the ground out from under me with Kit!*

He drove swiftly. Passing the bank corner, he saw a rig moving into town on the side road from the north. With its yellow wheels and running-gear, he identified it at a glance. He knew his father and Lee would have recognized it, too, if they hadn't been so busily engaged in their conversation.

Stash whipped up the team. Beyond question, Jim Brett was in Powder City for a showdown; in some way he had learned about the Lafoon matter. It spelled trouble, and in big letters.

"Let it come!" Stash muttered to himself. "I've had enough of this fence straddling! The old man will have to jump my way or Brett's!"

CHAPTER
THREE

A Little Job for Sixto

Brett had dozed in his buggy as he rode along, knowing his team could be relied on to keep to the road. In the early hours of the night, driving along under the peaceful stars, he had tried to look at the Lafoon incident from every angle. Try as he would, he could find nothing to excuse Stash's conduct. That it would undoubtedly lead to further trouble with Ben and end any hope of doing business with him did not weigh so heavily on Brett as the fact that his authority had been flouted, to say nothing of the deceit with which Stash had tried to carry it off.

Though he had never married, Jim had maintained a home of his own in Powder City for years. When the new Cameron House was thrown open to the public he had given up his home and moved to the hotel, where he kept a suite of rooms that made his bachelor existence more comfortable.

He drove to the barn in the rear of the Cameron House this morning and put up his team. Even at this early hour it was a scene of activity, with a freighting outfit bound for one of the mining camps in the Big

Medicines being hitched. Travis Fane, the barn boss, had time for a word with Brett.

"I hadn't expected yuh back for a week yet, Jim. Young Lee Cameron's home. Came in on Number 12. Stash and Morg just druv by with him a few minutes ago. The boy looks fine."

"I'm glad to hear it," Brett said. "I understood Lee was expected."

There was some mail for him at the hotel, and a bundle of newspapers that had been accumulating in his absence. He carried them upstairs and, after a warm bath, went to bed and sat up, reading, until long after the town was astir. He knew it was Morgan Cameron's habit to be at the bank by eight o'clock. With Lee just home, he'd very likely come down later than usual this morning. Accordingly, Jim took his time over what was for him an unusually late breakfast.

Morg saw his partner step through the bank doors. He came out from behind his desk, a puzzled look furrowing his face. "What are you doing in town, Jim? According to what Stash told me, I figured you was at Kelly Crick today."

"It's time we had an understanding, Morg," was the abrupt yet quiet answer. "That's why I came in. Things can't go on this way any longer."

"Wal!" Morgan snorted indignantly. "I don't know what's got you so het up. What's happened? What's wrong?"

"It's Stash again. He's over his head for fair this time. Ben Lafoon says he'll kill the next Brett-Cameron

28

man he finds on his side of the fence, and if I know Ben at all, he'll be as good as his word."

There were other people in the bank. Morg found it advisable to lead his partner to his private office. Behind closed doors he heard Brett's tale of what had occurred on Lafoon's range.

"Have you got your facts straight?" he demanded, expressing neither condemnation nor approval of what had happened.

"I've been getting my facts straight for a long time. If those cows had been shot, or even rustled, it wouldn't have been any worse than giving Ben this slap in the face. Making him look cheap and having people laughing at him are things he can't stand. Money won't buy his range now."

"I don't know about that. I'll give Stash hell for this nonsense. But you're making too much of it, Jim. Lafoon will cool off and think twice before he starts any shooting war with us. He don't want to get too high and mighty with me. I've offered him half again as much as his place is worth. Maybe this will bring him to his senses."

"That's the very position I was afraid you'd take!" Brett rapped. He was suddenly angrier than Morgan Cameron had ever seen him. "It's just that attitude that's given Stash reason to believe he can do as he pleases. It was bad enough when he went against me openly; this time he went behind my back. The whole crew sat there last evening knowing I'd been kept in the dark, my authority defied. I don't propose to stand for any more of it. Where is Stash?"

"Home, sleeping."

"You get him down here, Morg; I'll be back. The three of us will sit down and thrash this out. Unless he can convince me that he'll play square and aboveboard in the future, he isn't going back to Grass Valley as foreman."

Morgan Cameron's eyes flamed. "Don't you take too much on yourself, Jim. I got something to say about how things are run."

"And so have I! I never thought we'd come to the parting of the ways, but if that's how it's to be, this is as good a time as any."

Morg rifled a glance at him that was all fury and suspicion. "What are you trying to do, get me where the hair is short? You know I don't want to go back on the range. You figuring I'll sell out to you?"

"No," Brett said flatly. "I'm too old to swing that load. If anyone does any selling it'll be me. My half of Grass Valley is the only thing I won't sell. I'll flip a coin to decide how we divide our other interests."

The blood drained away from Morg's cheeks under the tan. If the offer he had just heard was Brett's way of trying to freeze him out, it was a strange one. "Good heavens, Jim, don't tell me you've gone far enough in your mind to be ready to break up the partnership!"

"I've gone that far, Morgan." Brett got to his feet, his mouth set and determined. "When we can't shoot square with each other any longer it's time to quit. I'll be back in an hour. You have Stash here."

Brett marched out, his back as stiff as a ramrod. Morgan's glance followed him, his amazement greater than his wrath. It was hard to believe that this was the mild-tempered, soft-spoken Jim Brett with whom he had come up from nowhere.

"Been twenty years since he got his dander up like this!" he muttered, the wonder of it nailing him to his chair.

He sat there for minutes on end, trying to face the facts with the same stern realism that had carried him to the top of the ladder. He didn't have to waste time debating the idea of selling out to Jim; under no circumstances did he intend to dispose of his half interest in the Brett-Cameron Company. He was just as positive that he didn't want to buy Brett out. Not now. As recently as a year ago he had entertained that idea, his thought being that Stash would come along and prove himself capable of running the business. He had seen enough in the past ten months to cast grave doubt on Stash's ability to measure up to such a responsibility.

Never having had any use for Ben Lafoon, Morg found something humorous in disfiguring the man's stock with a skull and crossbones.

"He must be burned up for fair," he said to himself.

He gave little consideration to what Lafoon might do; his problem was more difficult than that. He had to save face and it was his own face this time. Right or wrong, and he knew Stash was wrong, he had to stand by him.

"He's a Cameron — my son," he muttered. "Pull him away from Grass Valley and put another man in his place and I wouldn't be able to hold my head up in the community again."

But that was only part of it; he had to placate Brett, work out some compromise that would satisfy him. Jim was being unreasonable, making a mountain out of a molehill. Morg could extract little comfort from that; over the years he had never known the man to back-track. Jim didn't put out his horns very often, but when he did all the iron that was in him came to the surface.

Chewing his mustache as he sat there wrestling with his dilemma, inspiration came to Morg. He'd send Lee to Grass Valley with Stash. Not as his assistant — that wouldn't work out; but Lee could make his headquarters there and just his presence would be a check on Stash. He wouldn't be there all the time; there was no telling where disease would strike B C cattle. But Grass Valley was centrally located in relation to the other Brett-Cameron ranches. It seemed an ideal arrangement. Stash wouldn't like it, of course.

Morgan brought his fist down on his desk with an emphatic bang, his decision made. He didn't care what Stash thought.

When a messenger had been dispatched to the house, Morg walked to one of the front windows of the bank and gazed up and down the street. He failed to see anything of Brett.

At the moment Jim was on his way to the Mexican quarter of the town, a basket of groceries on his arm. It was unthinkable to him to sit down and waste an hour doing nothing. That he could turn to something else with almost complete detachment while a matter of the gravest importance hung in the balance was characteristic of the man.

Visiting what Powder City contemptuously called Greaser Town was not unusual for Brett. At regular intervals he crossed the sagebrush flats to the row of hovels, most of them constructed of discarded railroad ties, along the river south of the bridge. The railroad company gave employment to most of the men, finding them efficient laborers in its section gangs; a few worked on the ranches.

Brett's destination was the fourth house in the row, the home of the widow of Ceferino Gartiez. Three years ago a fast freight had jumped the switch at Squaw Butte and plowed through a gang of track laborers, killing Gartiez and two others. Long before that Ceferino had worked on the stage line from Powder City to Lander. One winter night, at the Sand Springs station, the building had caught fire. Half a dozen men had been upstairs asleep, Brett among them. Gartiez had aroused them and got them out in time. Brett had never forgotten, and he never permitted more than four or five weeks to pass without appearing in Greaser Town with his basket of groceries. When Maria Gartiez unpacked the basket she was always sure to find a ten-dollar bill tucked in on the bottom.

On the flat near the river's edge, where the graze was good and Maria pastured two milch cows, a group of children were playing. They no sooner caught sight of Brett than they scampered around to the back of the house, yelling, "Mister Jim! Mister Jim!"

In the rear, facing the muddy Yellowhorse, a crude wooden awning extended from the house. Beneath it the earthen floor had been packed hard by countless bare feet. On pieces of patched-together chicken wire hop vines grew luxuriantly on the open sides of the porch, turning back the bright rays of the sun but not shutting out the breeze that was invariably stirring along the river.

Brett found Maria there, her numerous progeny clutching at her skirt. Two of the youngsters had been born since Ceferino's death, a circumstance which Brett put down to human frailty and excused as of little consequence. She was churning butter this morning.

"*Como!* It is really you, Mister Jim!" She dried her hands hurriedly on her apron. "The little one say you come; I am think they make joke with me."

Brett set the basket on the table and took her hand. "I am glad to see you, Maria. How do things go?"

"Good," she answered, giving him a smile and a coquettish toss of her head. She was middle-aged, and very thin, but she hadn't lost her allure. There was a strong Indian strain in her that was reflected in her flat features and high cheekbones.

"I'm glad to hear it," he said. "I thought I'd like to drink a glass of buttermilk, so I came down and brought a few things along."

It was what he always said, his way of making light of his charity. Maria understood. She gave his hand a warm squeeze and peeked into the basket.

34

"So many nice thing for us!" she exclaimed happily. "You very good man, Mister Jim. Every time I go in the church I say prayer for you."

Brett smiled. "I reckon I can stand a lot of praying."

She sent the children scooting and carried the basket into the house. When she returned she had glasses and a pitcher of buttermilk. She sat at the table with Jim.

"I got surprise for you," she said. "Big surprise." Her dark eyes were bright and luminous against her olive skin. "What you think?"

Brett shook his head.

"Miguel Salazar ask me to marry with him." She saw she had to explain. "Miguel is section boss."

Brett shook his head for the second time. "I don't know him. Will he make you a good husband, Maria?"

"*Quien sabe?* Who knows?" She lifted her shoulders in a shrug that eloquently described her uncertainty. "He has good job, Miguel. He get drunk sometime, like the rest. Mebbe he beat me a little. But so! Is his right if he's husband. Sometimes mebbe I — what you call turn him round my finger, too. No?" Her laughter was mischievous and musical.

"Reckon you can take care of yourself," Jim conceded.

He studied her as she refilled his empty glass. Her faults were many, but her virtues far outweighed them. Best of all he liked her forthrightness.

"What you think, Mister Jim? Shall I marry with Miguel?"

A thought occurred to Brett and he didn't hesitate about putting it into words. "Tell me, Maria, is Miguel Salazar the father of the two little ones?"

"*Si*," she answered without embarrassment.

Jim nodded with pontifical sternness. "You better marry him. It'll make things better for all of you. You tell him for me he isn't to give up his job and leave it to you to make the living. I'll be after him if he does."

Maria rocked with laughter. "I tell him for sure, Mister Jim!"

After they had sat there talking for some time Brett pulled out his watch, thinking Maria would take the hint that he had to leave. She only talked faster. Somehow Brett got the feeling that she was sparring for time; that she had something to say and didn't quite know how to voice it. It was a shrewd surmise; Maria had something she wanted to say to him and she was vainly trying to find a way to lead up to it. There was little subtlety in her, however, and when she knew she must speak she did it with all the directness he admired in her.

"Mister Jim — you and the Camerons have big trouble, eh?"

Coming from her, the question startled Brett. He gazed at her in undisguised surprise for a moment. "Why do you ask me such a question, Maria?"

"You know Sixto?" she inquired guardedly, and only after she had glanced about and assured herself that they were quite alone.

"Sixto Guerra?" Brett nodded yes. "I know him. What's that little gunman got to do with me?"

36

Guerra did his swaggering in the saloons and brothels under the hill. He had served two terms in the penitentiary at Laramie City for crimes committed in other parts of the state, once for robbery and another time for rustling. In Powder City he had always been on his good behavior, with nothing more serious than a number of minor infractions of the law against him. It was generally believed, however, that his gun was for hire.

"Sixto is bad man," said Maria, "everybody say."

"That's not answering me," Brett interjected. "You know you don't have to beat around the bush with me, Maria. What is it?"

"Young Cameron — the one they call Stash — the last time he was under the hill he make plenty trouble, smash up couple place, throw some of the girls in river. He get awful drunk."

This didn't come under the heading of news to Brett. But Maria pulled him up sharply the next moment.

"He is good friend with Sixto. He say purty quick he be boss of the ranches; his father going kick you out. Sixto tell me."

Brett's eyes narrowed grimly. He didn't like what he'd heard, but he refused to take it too seriously. "A man says a lot of things when he's drunk, Maria."

"*Si*," she agreed. "Sometime he say too much."

"Well, finish it," Brett urged, his concern real enough by now. "What did Stash say that's got you so worried?"

"He tell Sixto mebbe he have little job for him soon." Maria crossed herself with a little darting movement of her hand. "*Madre de Dios* spare me! Sixto kill me for sure if he think I say anything to you."

"Don't worry; it won't go any further," Jim assured her.

"Don't trust that Stash!" she warned. "You be careful, Mister Jim! Me, I think he's snake in sheep's clothes."

Brett fought off the shock of it. "It was the whisky talking, Maria. But even drunk, I didn't think he'd have anything like that on his mind. Things are certainly coming to a head."

He didn't offer to explain the remark. If he had needed anything to fortify him in his determination to stick to his guns with Morg, Maria's story supplied it. He got up to leave; he was due at the bank.

"You got this direct from Guerra, Maria?"

"*Si! Positivo!*" she exclaimed, her feelings hurt that he should question her word. "May an evil stroke of lightning smother me if I not speak the truth to you. Sixto, he come from same village as me in Sonora. Once a week he come here for bring his shirts for me to wash and iron. He set down and talk with me."

"I just wanted to be sure," Brett observed soberly. "How soon will you be getting married?"

"Purty quick, I think, before Miguel change his mind." A roguish smile touched her face.

"He won't change his mind; he knows you've got what he wants." Jim pulled out his purse. "Here's twenty-five dollars, Maria; you go up to Altmier's and buy yourself a dress and shoes and fix yourself up for the wedding."

It was too much for Maria. Tears of happiness and gratitude welled to her eyes and she threw her arms about him impulsively. Brett gave her a warm hug as she clung to him.

"You behave yourself now, Maria, before you get my temperature up," he said with mock severity. "I don't know how long I'll be in town, but I'll see to it that Frank Paldino sends down a keg of vino for the wedding."

He was on his way across the flats a few moments later. Unconsciously he shook his head, as if trying to throw off a bad dream. Though his relations with Stash had steadily worsened, it was incredible to him that they could have reached the point where his removal from the Brett-Cameron Company — by violence if necessary — was being contemplated. That Morgan Cameron was conniving with Stash to such an end was even more unbelievable.

Morg ain't in on this — unless he's had the wool pulled over his eyes, he told himself. *He might trim me out of a dollar quick enough, but he'd stop a long way short of hiring a gunslinger to cut me down.*

He couldn't understand Stash's slant, and it did not occur to him that anyone other than himself might be the object of the big man's enmity.

He must have got the idea long ago that I was standing in his way, when what I was hoping was that he'd learn the business and be able to step into my shoes. Jim continued to shake his head grimly. *That's water under the bridge now; he'll know in a few minutes exactly where I stand.*

He intended to confine himself to the clash with Ben Lafoon and say nothing about the alleged remarks to Sixto Guerra. He realized that Guerra could have invented his tale just to impress Maria.

It won't surprise me if that turns out to be the case, he thought. *I've got no evidence that Stash is thick with him.*

He was ready to let it go at that for the present and put it out of his mind. Before he could lay it away, however, a question confronted him that put an entirely different face on the situation. Guerra was a convicted rustler. When he had been found guilty, across the line in Fremont County, there had been ample evidence that he had committed many similar offenses. So far as was known, he had never taken toll from Brett-Cameron Company beef. But once a rustler, always a rustler, was still a good range axiom, often quoted by none other than Morgan Cameron himself. That being so, why was Guerra tolerated in Powder City? He had been there almost a year. Morg could have had him run out of town on ten minutes' notice.

"Someone's been using his influence — someone mighty close to Morg," Jim muttered tensely. "This is one thing I can settle to my satisfaction; if it's Stash, I'll know it before I'm through with him this morning."

A side road took him to the main thoroughfare. He was still a block from the bank when he heard himself hailed. "Jim! Uncle Jim!"

He looked up to see Lee Cameron hurrying across the street to him, a happy grin on his young face.

Suddenly Brett found himself rooted to the spot, his answering greeting drying up in his throat. A flash of understanding had whipped through him that made his blood run cold. Gone was any doubt of the meaning of what he had learned from Maria. He realized his only mistake had been in thinking that he was the obstacle Stash was planning to remove from his path. It was not he; it was Lee!

Jim saw it all so clearly now. Down through the years Stash had always hated his brother. His boyhood attempt to kill Lee was not an isolated instance of it. At the time the excuse had been offered for him that he was so enraged he didn't know what he was doing. But Stash's only regret was that he had failed.

It wasn't necessary to go back that far, however, to understand what was in his mind. No longer ago than last evening, when Old Stony had arrived at Grass Valley with news of Lee, Stash's reaction had said plainly enough that he resented and dreaded his brother's return. Fearful lest Lee be put over him, even the thought of having to take orders from the youngster enraged Stash, and the grinding realization in the back of his mind that someday he would have to share with Lee whatever Morg left fanned the flames of his bitterness.

Lee was halfway across the street. Brett tried to put a smile on his face for the boy's sake, but his thoughts were black and grim.

Stash will never get away with it, he promised himself. *I'll stop him if I have to kill him myself.*

CHAPTER
FOUR

Close Call

The greetings over, Brett gazed at Lee with a critical eye and found no reason in this instance for dissembling the pride and affection he felt for the youngster. He had fought for the boy, made it his business to see that he had his chance. Stash was right about that.

"You've changed some, Lee; you're a little older around the eyes. You can't tell how much a man knows by looking at him, but I reckon you haven't been wasting your time back there."

Lee grinned. "I've learned a few things, Uncle Jim. I can't promise I can look a sick cow in the face and know what to do about it every time, but I sure can shoot some six-syllable words at you."

They spoke for a minute or two, then Brett sobered suddenly. "I wish we were meeting on a happier occasion, Lee. I drove in about daylight, with plenty on my mind."

Lee nodded. "So I understand. I hear Stash has got in your hair."

Brett looked up, surprised. "He tell you?"

"No. Dad sent word to the house about an hour ago that he wanted Stash and me to come down to the bank at once. They had it hot and heavy. The less I have to say about it, the better, I suppose."

"Yes, you keep out of it," said Jim. "But I'm glad you know. I don't have to tell you that whatever trouble Stash has let us in for with Lafoon isn't what sticks hardest in my craw." He glanced at his watch. "I'll see you later, Lee. I'm overdue at the bank."

"I'll walk along with you," Lee answered. "Dad sent me out to find you."

They fell into step. It was like old times, Lee thought, walking up the main street of Powder City with Uncle Jim.

Morgan Cameron was waiting at the bank door. He saw them coming, and when Lee would have continued on to the hotel he waved him back.

"You're one of the outfit now," he said. "That entitles you to sit down with us and hear what's said. You don't object, Jim?"

"No," was the glum response. "I haven't anything to say that he shouldn't hear. But I don't want him drawn into this trouble, Morgan; this is between you and me and Stash."

Morgan Cameron jerked his head in a noncommittal nod and led the way to his office.

Stash sat there glowering, his heavy face dark with his thinking. He longed to tear into Brett. Every fiber in his being rebelled at being stood in the corner and punished like a ten-year-old boy who had been caught stealing an apple. But he realized he had got ahead of himself; that he wasn't ready for a head-on collision with Jim. The stormy session he had just finished with

44

his father left no doubt of that. Not being a fool, he knew it was up to him to back down, eat humble pie. It came hard to him, but he told himself that the stake he was playing for was worth whatever it might cost.

He held himself in for several minutes, listening in scowling silence to Brett's recital of what had happened. Unable to restrain himself any longer, he leaped to his feet, fuming.

"Save your breath, Jim! I've had it handed to me once already from the old man; I can't stand a second dose! Sure I cut Lafoon's fence and sent a couple boys over to decorate his cows with a running-iron. You got it straight from start to finish. Maybe it was a fool thing to do. But you don't have to make a mountain out of a molehill. Lafoon can't give us any trouble. If he tries to, so much the better!"

Stash swung around and faced his father. "You tell the law what to do in this county. If Ben Lafoon makes a move, you can fix it so he'll find himself out on the end of the limb. He'll be damned glad to let us have his ranch to square himself."

"That's the worst nonsense I ever heard out of you!" Morgan snorted, the unscrupulous nature of the suggestion in no way responsible for his indignation. "I couldn't get away with anything as raw as that! Those days are gone! Besides, Lafoon's got friends!" He turned to Brett. "Can't you see Ben and square this mess?"

"What's the point in squaring it if it's to be repeated the next time I turn my back? And it will be repeated. If not this, then something else. What happened yesterday wasn't an accidental bit of foolishness; it was planned. Stash wanted Ben to come back at him and give him an excuse for going after him with guns doing the talking. He's as much as admitted it." Brett shook his head. "No sir!" he said flatly. "Grass Valley is going to be run my way — not his! That's final, Morg; we can decide here and now how it's to be. If you feel you can't go along with me on that, the only thing left to do is to call all bets off and turn in our chips."

In the course of what he had said to Stash earlier that morning Morgan Cameron had not failed to repeat Jim's ultimatum. Hearing it from his father had seemed incredible enough to Lee, but to have Brett sit there and declare with his own lips that he was ready, if necessary, to break up the Brett-Cameron Company passed all belief.

Stash had called it a bluff on Brett's part. Old Morg knew it wasn't any bluff. And yet he protested now that Jim didn't mean it.

"You're just talking, Jim! You know we're going to go on like we always have. Stash admits he made a mistake. Ain't that enough for you?"

Brett shook his head. "It'll take a lot more than that to satisfy me. He's been bushwhacking at my authority for months. It's his attitude that's wrong; he's got the idea that you'll back him up no matter what he does."

To be compelled to take such a dressing-down was gall and wormwood to Stash. To have to take it in front of Lee made it doubly bitter. He was consumed with hatred, not only for Brett and Lee but for his father as well, holding the latter to blame for what he was

46

enduring. And yet he knew he had to knuckle under, or pretend to; all his scheming and plans for the future would have been for nothing if the stewardship of the Grass Valley ranch were taken away from him.

"Reckon I had this coming to me," he acknowledged with a surly growl. "You can pile it on as much as you please, but the worst you can say is that I let the job go to my head. I know how you handle Bill Morrow and the other foremen; they can't dot an *i* or cross a *t* without your okay. I figured I was entitled to a little more leeway. But you get this straight, Jim: I haven't been running to the old man to get him to pull any chestnuts out of the fire for me; I've got more hell from him than I'll ever get from you."

To acknowledge his mistakes and in the same breath protest his innocence of the very thing that was the backlog of all his scheming was an ingenious procedure. He didn't make the mistake of protesting too loudly. He knew he was crawling, and he promised himself he would collect for it, and with interest, before he was finished.

"If you don't want me to use my own judgment when something comes up, it's all right with me. I can toe the line like any other hired hand. You give the orders, Jim, and I'll carry them out. You won't have any more trouble with me."

This was such a complete reversal of his usual attitude that Morgan Cameron couldn't conceal his amazement. Brett wasn't impressed.

"I wish I could believe that, Stash. If you could hold to it, you'd be a top man for the outfit. You're a hard worker when you put your mind to it; in spite of all the mistakes you've made, you've got Grass Valley showing a nice profit. I've got no complaints to make on that score." Jim was only trying to be fair, not wavering. "I told your father you weren't going back to the ranch unless you could convince me you were ready to play square and aboveboard in the future. That still goes — even if it means the breaking up of the Brett-Cameron Company. The good intentions you express may be something more than talk, but you'll have to prove it."

"Good grief!" Morg burst out fiercely. "What more do you want the man to do? He's admitted he was wrong and gives you his word he won't overstep himself again. I'll add my word to his. You won't have any more trouble with Stash. When he goes back to the valley Lee will go with him."

It took his sons, as well as Brett, by surprise. Stash was ready to explode in a second.

"I'll be damned if there's going to be two foremen at Grass Valley! You can't run an outfit that way."

"I didn't say nothing about two foremen!" Morg retorted with equal vehemence. "You'll ramrod the ranch; Lee will just make his headquarters there. He can fix up a room for an office. Chances are, when he's needed at one of the other ranches he'll be needed in a hurry. Six to eight hours' riding from Grass Valley will take him wherever he may have to go."

"And in the meantime he can keep tabs on me, eh? Is that your idea?"

"Mind your business and there'll be no need to keep tabs on you," Morg rapped. "What have you got to say about it, Jim?"

Brett was slow to answer. There were some things about the idea that appealed to him. It was true that Grass Valley was centrally located. Just how Lee was to apply himself he didn't know, but he took it for granted that his activity wouldn't be limited to doctoring ailing livestock. Then, too, his presence on the ranch would very likely have a restraining effect on Stash, and without Lee's having any thought of spying on his brother.

But there were other considerations that made Jim hesitate. He took it for granted that there would be strife between Stash and Lee. That it would sharpen Stash's enmity and strengthen him in his determination to put Lee out of his path was to be expected. It didn't necessarily follow that it would lead to a gory climax.

Throwing them together might be the best way to tie his hands, Brett told himself. *Stash won't try anything if he knows it can be pinned on him.*

"You going to take all morning to make up your mind?" Morg demanded impatiently.

"No, I've thought it over," said Jim. "If Stash wants to get the chip off his shoulder and go back to the ranch with Lee, I'm willing to give it a trial. I don't know how it'll work out, but we'll start with a clean slate; no grudges. I'll see Lafoon and try to pacify him. I expect he'll kick up his heels and do something to show us he doesn't have to take our backwash.

49

Whatever he does, Stash, I want you to overlook it. You understand?"

Stash nodded. "I'll walk wide of him." He felt he had won, and he was ready to promise anything. "If you ain't got nothing further to say, I'll be moving along; I've got a couple things to tend to before I head back to the valley."

Brett signified that he had no more to say.

"You be at the house for dinner," Morg told Stash. He also felt the argument had been resolved to his satisfaction. "Don't keep your mother waiting."

Stash turned at the door to glance at Lee. "When will you be showing up at the ranch?"

"Depends on how long it'll take me to get a few things together. I'd like to fix a little laboratory at Grass Valley. I don't know how far Jim and Dad will let me go."

"You can have whatever you want, as far as I'm concerned," said Brett.

Morg nodded. "Get anything you need. We'll go the whole way with you."

"You better be careful; you don't know what you're letting yourselves in for," Lee declared laughingly. "Before the summer gets very far along I'd like to have a dipping-tank at every one of the ranches."

"Dipping-tank?" Stash queried jeeringly. "You mean to tell me you're going to dip cattle the way they do sheep?"

"I want to be ready to dip them if we run into a siege of Texas fever." Lee saw that his father and Brett were as nonplused as his brother. "Dipping cows may sound crazy, but it'll save them if you can douse them in time. I'm not giving you a theory; I'm talking proved facts. Kill the ticks, and we won't have any Texas fever."

Old Morg shook his head. "I can't believe dipping alone will do the trick. It's the ticks that spread the fever, sure enough. They drop off a sick cow and get mashed in the grass. Turn healthy stock on that range and they eat the stuff. That's how they get the fever; and that's why it spreads so quick. And I figure the dung and saliva from a sick critter help to poison the graze. I don't see how dipping will get around that. Do you, Jim?"

"I don't know," Brett observed. "For forty years I've been trying to come up with the right answer, and I haven't got it yet. Back in the days when we didn't have anything but Texas cattle in this country, we didn't have any amount of tick fever. Cows would die, but it was never anything serious. Then we began getting white faces, pure-bred northern stock, and the epidemics began. We blamed it on the longhorns; but we saw the last of them eight or ten years ago, and we've got more tick fever than ever. So it couldn't have been the longhorns."

"But it was; they were carriers, Uncle Jim." Lee was emphatic in his knowledge. "You don't see any more longhorns in Wyoming, but stockmen are still bringing in southern cattle, aren't they?"

"Naturally." Stash's retort was contemptuous. He had little interest in the argument and remained only to scoff. "Their ribs are showing when we get 'em, but they put on fat and make good beef steers; and they don't turn up their toes and die of tick fever — not many of them."

"Of course they don't," Lee agreed. "They're immune; they had the fever when they were calves, and survived it. They may be crawling with ticks, but the bugs can't hurt them. It's a different story when the females drop off and lay their eggs, a couple thousand at a clip. In about three weeks those eggs are hatched and the young ticks lie waiting like a gang of murderers, ready to crawl up the legs of your Herefords. That's how the disease is spread. Ticks don't flit around like flies; they live their whole life on a cow. The males are dead when they drop off, and the females die as soon as they've laid their eggs. As for dead ticks, you could feed them by the pound to healthy stock and they'd grow fat on them."

Lee checked himself and glanced around at his audience. "I better stop," he said. "I could sit here the rest of the morning talking Texas fever. I don't suppose you've ever heard of Dr. Theobald Smith, of Cornell. I'm sure Professor Mosby has. Theo Smith is the best friend a stockman ever had; he's knocked all the mystery out of Texas fever. He's proved it can be controlled just the same as rinderpest and blackleg. I know I'm a greenhorn, without any practical experience, but I've got a great man to follow."

"Wonderful!" Stash declared sarcastically. It exasperated him to see his father and Brett taking Lee so seriously. "I was afraid you'd come home with a lot of big ideas. Sounds like we'll be chasing our tails before the summer's over."

He didn't remain to hear any more. Morg let him go without comment. Though he had never been one to accept advice or opinions that ran contrary to his own ideas on a matter, it pleased him to have Lee speak out with such authority and conviction. If what the boy had to say ran contrary to his own belief, it was all right with Morg; he had footed the bills for those four years at Cornell and he expected them to pay some dividends. But building dipping-tanks at Grass Valley and the rest of the ranches was going to cost money, and after they were completed the expense would continue; dipping thousands of cows would be a job. It meant that the crews would have to be kept at full strength during the slack summer season.

Brett was thinking much the same thing. "Suppose we try out the idea at Grass Valley before we go ahead at Kelly Creek or anywhere else," he suggested. "If it works, it'll be the best investment we ever made."

"It'll work, Uncle Jim." There was no room for doubt in Lee's mind. "Wait until I get a microscope set up, I'll show you how the ticks work. They produce a microbe that attacks the blood and breaks up the corpuscles. The germ gets right inside the blood cells. That's why a cow gets a violent anemia and dies."

They sat there for nearly fifty minutes, fascinated by what he had to say but finding it somehow incredible.

The cashier rapped on the door and had a whispered word with Morg.

"I'll be through here in a minute," Cameron informed him. "You tell Henry to wait." And to Lee he said, "I knew you wouldn't come home empty-headed.

53

They say there's always something new coming up. Maybe you've got the right answer. When you get ready to make some experiments you let me know. I want to come out to the valley and see 'em. I know Jim will string along with you and give you anything you want. The two of you will have to get out of here now and let me catch up with the morning's work. I'd like to ask you up to the house for dinner, Jim, but Mattie ain't feeling at all well."

"So I understand," said Brett. "You tell her to take things easy. I'll fiddle around town for an hour or two and pull out for Kelly Creek. I'll see Ben before I get back to town. In the meantime, if he comes into the bank, try to placate him, Morg. It'll only aggravate him if you say anything about buying him out. He's in no mood to sell now. A little later we may talk him into letting us have his south range, that three thousand acres below Buckshot Creek."

"It ain't likely he'll come in. If he does, I'll let him blow off steam," Morg promised.

Brett and Lee left the bank together. On the sidewalk they paused for a parting word. On the opposite corner two men stepped out of the store-front-building that housed the Powder City *Gazette* and began a violent argument. One of the men was Buck Close, who conducted a saloon and dance hall under the hill. The other was Sixto Guerra. Sixto was seldom seen uptown this early in the day.

Brett thought it strange. The argument the two were having seemed to concern a woman. "You're lying, Sixto!" Lee and Jim heard Close snarl. "I don't care what you say, I know you been seeing her! I'm telling you for the last time, I won't stand for it!"

He stepped off the sidewalk and started diagonally across the street for the bank corner. Guerra stood watching him intently. Close, a big man, his shoulders hunched, didn't look back, but when he was halfway over he whirled suddenly and whipped up a gun.

Sixto seemed to have expected nothing less, and before Buck could fire Sixto slapped a shot at him, squeezing the trigger a split second after he had his gun out of the holster. It was a wild shot. The slug missed Close by a wide margin and pinged off the brick front of the bank within inches of Lee Cameron's head.

It was enough for Close, however. He threw down his gun, and Sixto turned away with a sneering laugh. The incident had taken no longer than it does for a man to draw a deep breath.

There had been a score of witnesses, Shad Childress, the town marshal, among them. Shad came running. Ignoring Close for the moment, he caught up with Sixto and whirled him around.

"What's the idea?" he growled. "You know you can't get away with gunplay on the main street of this town, Guerra!"

Shad had been keeping the peace, according to Morgan Cameron's dictates, for a good many years. Though he could look the other way when the occasion demanded, he had plenty of iron in him and had proved it innumerable times.

"He drew on me," Sixto protested. Shad's presence didn't seem to disturb him. "You'll give me the right to defend myself, won't you?"

"I don't give a dang about your rights!" was the angry answer. "Take your troubles under the hill where they belong and nobody will bother you. For the fancy gun slinger you claim to be, your shootin' stinks — if it was Buck you was tryin' to drop."

It pulled Guerra to his toes. "What do you mean by that?" he demanded, all his easy indifference gone.

Shad's narrowed eyes drilled into Sixto. "You know what I mean," he muttered cryptically. "That wild slug came in inches of killin' Morg Cameron's boy."

Buck Close had picked up his gun and would have stolen away. Shad called him back.

"I'm takin' the two of you in for disturbin' the peace," he announced. "Start walkin'. I'll be right behind you."

Over at the bank Lee fingered the chipped brick where the slug had struck.

"That was a near accident for me," he said. "About the closest call I ever had."

Brett nodded soberly. "It was close. I'm not sure it was an accident."

Lee gazed at him, completely puzzled. "I don't get you, Uncle Jim."

"I might have been mistaken," Brett replied, "but I thought that shot was deliberately wild." After a moment's hesitation he said, "You're not back in New York State now, Lee. You used to know how to handle a .45. If you'll take my advice, you'll start packing a gun."

56

CHAPTER
FIVE

New Ideas for Old Heads

The little building that housed the observation station on the Painted Meadows stood back several hundred yards from the road. Not so many people passed in the course of a day that Kit Mosby failed to notice who was coming and going.

Whenever anyone turned in she always had a minute or two in which to powder her nose and tuck a stray wisp of hair into place before going to the door to greet a visitor.

She and her father had been home three days, and had fallen back into the routine ways of their lives, when she saw a light wagon, drawn by a pair of bay ponies, moving along the road from Powder City. The driver of the rig, the sole occupant, was not recognizable at that distance. When he slowed his team to a walk, as he neared the entrance to the station, and proceeded to turn in without any hesitation, her curiosity wasn't to be denied. Getting up from the table where she was typing, she stepped into her bedroom and spent a moment or two at the mirror. By the time she got to the front door the visitor was within hailing distance. With a little rush of excitement she saw that it was Lee Cameron. Under a wide Stetson, and wearing a gun belt, he seemed an older and much more determined young man than he had appeared on the train.

"Mr. Cameron!" Kit exclaimed happily. "It's a pleasure to see you again so soon."

"I hope it's not too soon," said Lee, a merry light in his gray Cameron eyes. "I said I'd stop in the first time I found myself in the meadows. I thought I'd be as good as my word."

"It's not a bit too soon," she assured him. "You must have left town early."

"I did. I'm on my way to Grass Valley."

There was a bench beside the door. Kit invited him to sit there with her, explaining that it was cooler outside than inside this morning.

"Father will be sorry to have missed seeing you," she said. "He's sound asleep; it was a clear night for his work and he was up till almost dawn."

She asked Lee about his mother and was pleased to hear that Mrs. Cameron was feeling better. "Having you home is the best medicine she could get," she said. "Your mother is very fond of you, Mr. Cameron."

"Lee is the name," he corrected her banteringly.

"And Kit," she said in the same tone.

She was wearing a pair of many times washed Levis and a man's shirt. Lee recalled what his father had said on the subject and found himself agreeing with him; Kit Mosby didn't need ruffles and furbelows to hold a man's eye.

He told her about what he planned to do at the ranch. "It won't be much of a laboratory — not at first, at least — but I'll set up a microscope and have a little something to work with."

The interest Kit expressed was genuine. "This range country can use some practical scientific knowledge. It sounds like a great opportunity for you. I hope we'll be seeing you now and then; Grass Valley isn't too far away."

"No, not as we count miles," he agreed. "I'll be getting around. With your permission, you'll be seeing me."

Kit laughed. "The latchstring's always out. I suppose you know Vangie Edwards and the other girls over Deep Springs way."

"I used to know them. Is Vangie's hair as red as ever?"

"It's red — and beautiful. I don't know what I'd do without Vangie. She and the Comerford girls are arranging the last spring dance of the year at the Deep Springs schoolhouse a week from Friday. Will you be there?"

"Will you?" Lee countered.

Kit said yes. "Stash stopped by the other day and asked me to go."

It pulled down the corners of Lee's mouth, but he didn't hesitate over his answer. "If you'll save a dance for me, I'll be there."

"That's a promise," Kit said lightly. "I'll tell Vangie you're coming. She'll be over this afternoon."

Though he was certain that he was about to add to his difficulties with Stash, Lee put it out of his mind until he was on his way north again.

"I might have known it," he mused. "What I saw at the train the other morning should have told me how things stood." He shook his head over it. "I'm not going to let it make any difference to me. I want to get along with Stash; I'm willing to back down to him on some things. But that doesn't go where she's concerned."

Lee found that his brother had made no preparations for his coming, so on his own initiative he had Oddie Williams, the ranch's handy man and cook's swamper, clean out one of the front rooms. Between them, they built some shelves and set up a worktable. By evening, when Stash came in with the crew, Lee had things arranged the way he wanted them.

"So this is what you call a laboratory, is it?" Stash queried, looking over the rack of test tubes and rows of bottles. There were several sterilizing-jars on the table, as well as a microscope.

"It'll do until I can get something better," said Lee. "I'm going to bunk in here, too. If I want to work at night, I can do it without disturbing anybody."

Stash gave him a glance that was filled with a vague hostility. "Didn't Oddie tell you Jim uses this room whenever he stays here overnight? Or maybe Jim won't mind being pushed out. Anything you do seems to be all right with him."

The insinuation was too pointed to be ignored.

"That's no way for us to start, Stash," Lee said. "I know you don't want me here, but we've got to manage

60

to get along together. I'm ready to lean over backward to do it."

"Don't strain yourself," Stash grumbled. "Everything will be okay if you'll just remember that I'm bossing this outfit. And be damned sure you don't step on my toes!"

There were some old B C riders in the Grass Valley crew, men like Joe Ryan, Reb Sanders, and Top Laneer. They remembered Lee and were glad to see him. Duke Rucker, Bill Dent, and several others were new. They greeted the youngest of the Cameron clan with blank faces and a cool restraint that was neither friendly nor unfriendly, as far as the eye could tell. But Lee had the feeling that evening at supper, and later events were to confirm it, that the big crew was sharply divided into two camps, with the old hands loyal to the brand and Jim Brett rather than willing to go the whole way with Stash.

Stash and Lee sat at the table after the men went out. Where the dipping-tank was put in seemed to be of no importance, but Lee purposely asked his brother to pick out a location.

"Then you're actually going to build it?" Stash demanded disparagingly.

"I've got a hundred bags of cement and a load of rough lumber for the concrete forms on the way up," Lee told him. "They ought to be showing up tomorrow."

"By damn, if that don't take the cake!" was Stash's growling response. "Jim has me turning handsprings to save a dollar, yet he and the old man let you talk them into throwing money away! You expect my crew to build your tank?"

"No, I've got some Mexican laborers coming. They can do the job in three or four days. Why are you so down on the idea, Stash?"

"Because it gravels me to see a kid coming home from college and telling men who've spent their lives in this business that they don't know anything about it. You can build your tank wherever you damn please. Just be sure you locate it far enough away from the house so we won't smell your stinking creosote all night."

Lee let it go at that. In another month, following its usual custom, the Brett-Cameron Company would be shipping in several thousand head of southern cattle. When the real hot weather came, and the ticks began dropping, he was satisfied that Stash would have to sing a different tune.

He waited for his brother to make some reference to the dance at the Deep Springs schoolhouse. Stash didn't mention it, however, and Lee said nothing about having stopped at the station on his way up to the ranch.

He had to have riding stock.

"I'd like to have a little string of my own," he told Stash. "I don't need anything fancy."

"I don't know what you call fancy. We've got some good broncs running free in the lower meadow. I'll tell Duke to go down with you in the morning and cut out whatever you want. There's a big white-faced sorrel down there that'll make you a good top horse." Stash got up and moved to the door. Over his shoulder, he said, "They're apt to be a little rough. If you don't feel up to knocking the edges off them, I'll have the boys do it for you."

Lee got the thrust. "I'll get along without any wet nursing; I haven't forgotten how to fork a bronc."

The laborers and material for building the dipping-tank arrived the next day. It was to be nothing more than a deep trough, with a ramp leading down into it at both ends.

Lee got busy at once. He had to take some good-natured joshing from the old hands, who had seen him grow up from the short-pants stage.

"You figgerin' to delouse some of the two-legged critters on this ranch as well as the cows?" Top Laneer inquired with a straight face.

Lee laughed. "You think they need it, Top?"

"Inside as well as out, if you ask me," Top returned. "It ain't their smell I object to so much as what goes on inside their skulls. Reckon that would be purty hard to git at."

"Reckon it would," Reb Sanders agreed. He had grown old and bald-headed working for Jim Brett and Morg Cameron. His shrewd, homely face was usually expressionless, but no man liked a laugh better than he. "How you aimin' to git your cows into this contraption, Lee?"

"I'll drive them in through a chute. When we get the trick of it, we'll be able to run a couple hundred head a day into the tank."

Reb shook his head pessimistically. "Mebbe you will! But by gravy, I don't want to be on the other end when they come bustin' out! They'll have their tails up and be sprayin' carbolic or creosote all over this ranch!"

"They'll be spooky," Lee admitted. "Just get them headed in the right direction, Reb, and they'll get where they're going in a hurry."

Little Tiny Duprez joined the circle. "I got this thing all figgered out," was his weighty observation. "This ain't no dippin'-tank Lee's buildin'; it's a mantrap. He's gittin' everythin' set so that when Ben Lafoon and his lads come bustin' in here some night they'll take a header into his ditch and git drownded."

It won the heartiest laugh of the morning. It was good to hear men laugh again, Lee thought. In the old days there had been plenty of laughter at Grass Valley.

Top and the others swung into the saddle and rode off. Tiny's mention of Ben Lafoon was the first reference Lee had heard anyone make to him. A week had passed since the invasion of Ben's range. Since he had attempted no reprisal, Lee surmised that Brett had managed to placate him.

His feeling that the incident was closed gradually began to be shared by the crew as the days continued to pass peacefully. And then one morning, just before dawn, there was a furious rattle of gunfire in the yard. Slugs spattered the house and shattered three or four windows.

Stash came running down the stairs, his shirttails flapping. Everyone was aroused, trying to keep out of the line of fire as they pulled on their britches. There wasn't any doubt as to who was doing the shooting.

"It's Lafoon's bunch!" Stash yelped, saying only what everyone knew. "Quarter up to the windows and get your guns bucking!"

He had snatched up a pair of .45s. Running to the kitchen door, he rushed out into the yard.

He was too late; the shooting had ended as abruptly as it had begun. Only the pounding of retreating hoofs greeted him. He emptied his guns aimlessly in their direction and came stamping back into the house.

"Don't no one strike a light!" he barked. "Open the windows and be ready for 'em if they come back! We'll blast hell out of them if they do!"

"They had their fun; they won't be back," Duke Rucker growled. The others had nothing to say.

The sky began to lighten before long. Stash held the crew indoors until it was full dawn. He led the way outside then, to inspect the damage. It amounted only to shattered windows and a bullet-pocked door. Stash forgot all about the house when Tiny Duprez called his attention to the clothesline on which the cook's swamper dried his towels. Draped over the line was the hide of a B C steer, and burned thereon, and with some art, was the picture of a man thumbing his nose at the big B C brand.

By comparison, the pointedness and artistry of the insult put Stash's foray on Lafoon's cows completely in the shade. Tiny, Laneer, and a few others found some humor in the situation. But not Stash; the boot was on the other foot now, and it pinched him painfully. Beside himself, he ordered the hide hauled down and buried at once.

"Lafoon will hear from me!" he raged. "I'll show him we can throw some lead too! It'd serve him right if we tossed a few sticks of dynamite in Buckshot Creek and blocked it off! That would leave him high and dry! If I —"

He checked himself as he caught Lee regarding him soberly. "I forgot you were around," he snapped. "What have you got to say about it?"

"You asked for what you got," Lee replied. "Jim told you Lafoon would hit back."

"So what?"

"You gave Dad and Jim your word you'd steer clear of Lafoon. But you're on your own; do as you please."

Lee turned away and left him standing there.

After breakfast Stash rode east with the fencing-wagon and half a dozen men to work along Buckshot Creek. Lee heard no gunfire during the day, but that night there was a grass fire on Lafoon's range, and he surmised that it was of incendiary origin.

Work on the tank progressed, and early the following week it was finished. Jim Brett arrived at Grass Valley two days later. He listened to Stash's story of the raid.

"That tallies with what Ben told me," he said. "I had a long talk with him this morning. He says you set his range afire."

"He's a liar," Stash protested. "I hope you didn't let him get away with that."

"I'm only telling you what he thinks. His grudge is against you personally. He said if I wanted to talk

66

business with him, I'd have to pull you off of Grass Valley first. The only thing I could do was to tell him I didn't intend to have him or anyone else telling me how this outfit was to be run. So, I guess we can forget all about making any sort of a deal for his south range." Brett's tone indicated how deeply he regretted the fact.

"About the time you hit town with your calf crop the stuff bought down in New Mexico will be showing up. There's twenty-two hundred yearling steers in the lot. You won't be able to take many of them on here without more range."

"We can handle three or four hundred head," said Stash.

Brett nodded. "That'll be about all . . . You planning to take in the dance at Deep Springs?"

Stash straightened up, surprised at the question. "What makes you ask?"

"Ben's been making the rounds with his story. He's stirred up some feeling against you. He's even got Charlie Edwards on his side, and that surprised me a little. Charlie and your father have always been pretty thick."

Stash jerked a nod. "I'm glad to have the information, Jim. I don't care how much feeling there is against me; it won't keep me away."

Brett examined the dipping-tank and had a long talk with Lee. "You've got everything ready in good time," he remarked. "I've made a swing around all our ranches and never found the stuff looking better."

"It's early, Uncle Jim. July will be the test of what we're in for this year."

"I know it," Brett agreed. "I just finished telling Stash I'd have three, maybe four hundred head of New Mexican stock for him in about ten days. As I understand it, it's just the new stuff you intend to dip."

"For a beginning," Lee replied. "I want to run every one of these southern cows through the tank before they're turned out to grass. I'll watch our home-bred stock carefully. When a cow stops eating and begins standing around with its back humped, it's going to get dipped in a hurry. Have you passed the word to all our foremen that they're to get in touch with me at the first sign of Texas fever?"

"I've left them in no doubt about that. The symptoms are always unmistakable. It'll give you a little warning. But I don't know what you can do if a bunch of cows take sick as far away as Kelly Creek or Twin Buttes. You can't drive fever-ridden stock a hundred miles."

"No, they'd die before I got them here," said Lee. "Shooting anti-toxins into them wouldn't help any. I'll segregate them and try a spray gun. I'm not afraid of any epidemic at Grass Valley. By the time another summer rolls around I'll have a suggestion for you that you'd laugh at if I made it now."

"Huh!" Brett exclaimed with a chuckle. "Is that so? What is it?"

"Move every cow off this range and bring in all the new stuff you're buying. I could dip the whole bunch in a week. This fall I could run them through again. We might get some fever at the other ranches, but it wouldn't be serious. I'll guarantee you we wouldn't have any here to amount to anything."

Brett shook his head incredulously. "Good grief, Lee, that would be some undertaking! Do you realize how much work it would mean? We couldn't do it now even if we wanted to; we'd be moving stock all summer, to say nothing about how it sets cattle back to take them off range they're accustomed to and put them on new graze. If we ever get around to doing what you suggest, we'll have to make a lot of advance preparations. The time to start would be late in the year, after the roundup and the fall shipping."

Lee could only acknowledge that this was true. "But once started, we'd stick to it," he declared. "We'd funnel every head of new stock through Grass Valley."

They spoke of other things. Jim asked if Lee had been over the ranch.

"Several times," was the answer. "I found some dangerous patches of wild parsnip along the creek. The tops are pure poison for livestock this time of the year. Stash sent a couple men out to burn the stuff. Tiny came down from the big coulee day before yesterday with news that we had some cows weaving around, plumb loco. I went back with him and Top. From what Tiny had to say, I figured the cows had got into some fit weed; and sure enough, they had. An old red bull was down, and pretty sick. I gave him a stiff hypo. We moved the other stuff out of the coulee and dug up as much of the weed as we could. The only reason it's showing up is because the coulee's being overgrazed."

"That's true, I reckon," Brett agreed. "You can understand why I was so anxious to do business with Lafoon."

They walked back to the house together.

"How are you and Stash hitting it off?" Jim asked.

"About as you'd expect. I keep out of his way as much as possible. We'd get along all right if he could get the idea out of his head that I'm trying to double-cross him."

That hit the nail squarely on the head, as Brett saw it. He stole a glance at Lee. *This youngster has a lot of savvy in him*, he told himself.

"Walking around a situation never cures it," he said, choosing his words carefully. "Sooner or later you'll have to stand up to Stash. It'll have to be a real showdown. When it comes, it will either clear the air or make you sworn enemies for the rest of your lives."

He didn't mind having had his bed moved to an upstairs room. "Down here was the proper place for you to set yourself up," he told Lee.

That evening he sat down to supper with the crew and the brothers. As far as the men were concerned, the tension and preoccupation that had rested on them so heavily during his last visit were largely gone. But the rough good-fellowship he liked to see in his crews was missing.

The work gets done, but they're not pulling together, he said to himself. *Stash can't be handling them right*. He was placing the blame where he was sure it belonged. He didn't expect B C men to grow into plaster saints or always see eye to eye. They'd quarrel. A good foreman would see that they got over it, or he'd fire them.

Without seeming to, he studied Stash and Lee as they ate, listening to their conversation and putting in a word or two of his own. He didn't have to look very far beneath the surface to find blind, unreasoning hatred in one and a quiet determination to stand up for his rights in the other. At best, there was only an uneasy truce between them, made possible only because Lee had chosen to give ground.

There'll be a point beyond which he won't go, Brett mused, *and then they'll meet head on. And it's coming sooner than either of them realizes.*

CHAPTER
SIX

Storm Clouds

Brett always decided what percentage of the company's calves were to be marketed. He gave Stash the quota for Grass Valley, and the next morning the gather began. The little fellows were driven in and corralled until they were to be trailed to town and the railroad.

The work usually took three or four days. It proceeded satisfactorily, and when Stash passed the word that the drive to Powder City would get away from the ranch at daybreak Sunday morning, just missing interfering with the dance at the Deep Springs schoolhouse, the crew's table talk immediately became concerned with who was going to the dance and what girls were likely to be there.

Little Tiny was one of the first to announce he'd be among those present. He seldom missed a dance. After being in the saddle all day, he thought nothing of riding as much as forty miles to, as he put it, "shake a leg" for an hour or two, even though it took him the rest of the night to get back to the ranch. Deep Springs was only fifteen miles away, just a pleasant jaunt for him.

"How about you fellas?" he asked Top and Reb.

"I'll take it in," said Top. "It's the last shindig till fall. I hear old Corry's going to be there; he's a mighty good fiddler."

Reb said no. "You can count me out; I ain't interested in watchin' you Fancy Dans showin' off. I know you'll be the life of the party. After you've stopped at the Ford and put away three or four hookers of Slick Peasant's rat poison, there won't be no holdin' you down."

"How you talk!" Tiny gave Reb a pained look. "I don't need none of Slick's snakebite to wind me up. But you don't mind stoppin' at Lundy's Ford just to be sociable, do you?"

"I'm allus willin' to be a sociable cuss," said Reb, "but I ain't goin' up against the kind of sociable stuff Slick hands out. I'd liefer drink some of Lee's cow dip. You talk Dex Ferris and Ryan into goin' with you, and leave me out."

"We don't have to talk nobody into goin'," Tiny informed him caustically; "we can go alone."

"Sure!" Reb acknowledged. "I was just thinkin' you might run into an argument at the Ford," he added, the levity gone from his tone. "Chances are you'll bump into some of Lafoon's Tumble L lads."

Through the window he could see Rucker, Bill Dent, and Hank Morell with their heads together.

"They'll be goin'," said Reb, "and that won't help matters."

Tiny would have brushed it all aside, but Top said, "Reb's right. If he won't go, we'll make Joe and Dex tag

73

along with us. In case somethin' comes up, we'll be able to settle it."

Through the years various arguments had been settled at Lundy's Ford, the only good crossing on the upper Yellowhorse in ten miles. In the eighties Pete Lundy had squatted there and given the place its name. The building he had put up, now a weather-beaten, scabious-looking structure, was still the only one there. In it he had conducted a back-country saloon and grocery. The business had changed hands many times since Pete had given up on it and drifted out of the country, for though no one had ever been able to make a living out of it someone always turned up and took it over.

With each new owner the reputation of Lundy's Ford became worse. Slick Peasant, a shifty, gimlet-eyed French Canadian, had been there for the past two years. It was generally suspected that he helped himself to other men's beef at times, but though he was regarded as an unsavory character he was considered harmless, beyond a little petty thieving.

Just after breakfast on Wednesday, Lee was called to the Kelly Creek ranch. Some horses had got tangled up in barbed wire and needed attention. He was back at Grass Valley on Friday morning. He was not surprised when Stash came in early that afternoon and ordered old Oddie to hitch a team to a buckboard.

Lee spoke to him briefly. Stash was so careful not to say anything regarding his plans for the evening that

Lee smiled to himself as he watched his brother climb the stairs to his room.

Must be that he's afraid I might beat his time with Kit, he thought. He was suddenly sober. *Maybe I can. If I don't, it won't be for lack of trying.*

Kit Mosby had often been in his mind since he had come to the ranch. He couldn't get over the fact that he had had to travel halfway across the country, be gone for years, and then come home to Powder City to find a girl who could quicken his pulse with the flash of her eyes and tighten his throat with longing.

Stash was upstairs a long time. When he came down he was freshly shaven and looked well scrubbed. In a white silk shirt, string tie, and tight-fitting black broadcloth pants he seemed taller and thinner than usual. In his hand he carried his gun belt and .45.

The cook had his supper on the table, though it was not yet five o'clock. As he sat there, Lee wandered in.

"Going to town?" he asked, putting the question in a way that made it sound innocent and aimless.

"I'm going to Deep Springs, to the dance," was the annoyed but surprisingly frank answer. "Who do you think you're fooling — asking me if I'm going to town? You know damned well I'm due to get the calves moving Sunday morning."

Lee was not satisfied with having smoked Stash out; he had to needle him a little.

"That's right, I'd forgotten all about the calves. I guess there'll be quite a few going over . . . You're getting an early start, aren't you?"

"I aimed to," Stash snapped. "Is it any skin off your chin when I go?"

Lee shrugged it off. "Not unless you want to make something of it," he said, his tone vaguely challenging. "If it's any news to you, I'm going over, myself, after supper. I'll see you there."

Stash had finished eating. Picking up his gun belt, he started out. Halfway to the door he swung around abruptly, his face hard. "If you're going over with the idea that you're going to cut hay at my expense, you want to forget it! If a certain party shows you any favors because you're my brother, don't let it go to your head!"

He stamped out, his shoulders hunched angrily. After concealing his guns in the folds of a blanket on the floor of the buckboard, he drove off.

The crew came in an hour later and hurriedly scrubbed up and got into their finery. As soon as supper was out of the way, Duke Rucker and three of his cronies pulled out for Deep Springs. In another fifteen minutes Tiny, Top, Dex Ferris, and Ryan were ready to leave. Lee went with them. He saw that they were armed.

"Why the guns?" he asked Tiny.

"We're packin' 'em just in case some of Lafoon's crowd may be waitin' for us at the Ford with blood in their eye."

"I doubt it," Lee told him. "I guess they pretty well know who cut their wire. I'm sure it wasn't anyone in this bunch."

76

"It was someone, sure enough," Tiny declared diplomatically. "They may mistake the sheep for the goats."

They jogged along without trying to overtake Rucker and the others. Though they were in no hurry, there was plenty of daylight left when they splashed across the Yellowhorse at Lundy's Ford. Half a dozen broncs stood at the hitch rail in front of the saloon. Top read the brands.

"All Tumble L," he muttered. "They're here. Reckon Rucker and his pals didn't stop."

"They scare purty easy," Tiny said pointedly. He flashed a glance at Lee. "We know these fellas from away back. We gotta stop and give 'em a chance to speak their piece, if they got anythin' on their minds."

Lee nodded. "That's the way I see it."

He had last seen Lundy's Ford during the summer following his freshman year at Cornell. In the three years that had intervened since then the rickety old building had developed a decided list. Wind had torn away more of the warped shingles. On the second floor, broken windows had been boarded up to keep out the snow and cold of winter.

Tiny led the way up to the rack. They tethered their broncs and climbed the wooden steps together. They found the six Tumble L riders standing with their elbows on the bar, facing the door. Tiny and the B C men jerked nods. Lafoon's crew returned them. Lee was the only stranger here. Behind the bar Slick Peasant looked on with vacant eyes. Tumble L wore its range clothes and obviously was not going to the Deep Springs dance.

Tiny looked them over, and the tension mounted.

"Wal, what's it to be, war or whisky?" he inquired.

Neph Gibson, a grizzled veteran, laughed. Ben Lafoon was his own foreman, but Neph was Ben's top hand. There was a long-standing friendship between Tiny and Neph.

"The little runt's still a yard wide and good on both sides," Neph declared. "I knew he wouldn't walk away from us . . . We wa'n't waitin' here for you boys, Tiny; it was Rucker and that other bunch we was aimin' to have some words with. They didn't choose to stop." He waved the B C men up to the bar. "We used to drink with you boys; I reckon we can still rub elbows."

Faces relaxed, and the tension was gone. Slick filled the glasses. Neph Gibson gave Lee a long glance. He knew him by sight.

"You're Stash Cameron's brother," he remarked.

That was all he had to say. It was enough. Lee felt a curtain drop between him and the Tumble L men. They had their sights trained on Stash and his clique, but for old times' sake they were willing to take down the bars for certain B C men. That didn't include him. He made a pretense of finishing his drink, since Tiny was paying for it, and then turned on his heel and walked out.

Tiny broke the silence Lee had left behind him. "You're wrong, puttin' on the ice for that boy; he's a square shooter."

"That may be, we ain't heard nothin' to the contrary," Gibson observed. "But he's a Cameron. That rules him out with us."

That put a period to the subject. The conversation turned to less controversial matters. Neph bought a round, and there was laughter and bantering along the bar.

"What'd you think of the way we dolled up that hide we left on your clothesline?" a Tumble L man inquired.

"It was purty good," Tiny acknowledged.

"It was damn' good!" Neph protested. "I bet it had Stash beatin' his gums. Where was he while all that shootin' was goin' on? Under the bed?"

"By grab, I dunno what he was doin', but you shore had the rest of us huggin' the floor."

They had another drink or two.

"That'll have to be all," said Tiny. "We got to be movin'."

Neph slapped him on the back and urged him to have another. The little man said no.

B C started out. Neph walked to the door with Tiny.

"It was nice cuttin' up a few old touches with you and the boys," he said, his manner suddenly grave. "It may be the last time. If Brett and old Morg don't yank Stash away from Grass Valley, this trouble is goin' to end with dead men. I can smell it."

"Could be," Tiny muttered. A thought crossed his mind and he looked Neph in the eye. "With so many of us off the ranch tonight, you ain't figgerin' on raidin' us, are you?"

"No, the next move is up to Stash. We ain't a big outfit, Tiny, but we got some good backin'. If you come at us, we'll shore be shootin' at you."

Lee swung up with the others, and they left the Ford behind them. Tiny moved up alongside him as they rode along.

"It took nerve to walk out on that bunch," the little man said. "They respect you for it."

"There wasn't anything else for me to do," Lee replied, tight of lip. "I don't propose to apologize for being a Cameron."

The dance had got off to an early start and was in full swing by the time they reached the schoolhouse. As usual there was a big crowd on hand; a score of rigs stood in the schoolyard, Stash's buckboard among them. Saddle horses lined the fence.

A table had been set up outside the door for the convenience of the gentlemen, and the schoolhouse cloakroom was reserved for the ladies' use.

Lee paused at the table to deposit his hat. Tiny and his companions unbuckled their gun belts and coiled them up in their Stetsons before handing the headgear over to Tom Sweet, a Deep Springs rancher, who was in charge.

"Tickets is four bits apiece," Sweet announced. "How many?" He was less friendly than usual.

"Five," said Lee. "My treat, boys," he told Tiny and the others.

At the door he ran into a man who was big and broad and unsmiling. This was Bill Morrow, the

80

foreman of the Brett-Cameron Company's Deep Springs ranch and long an important cog in B C operations.

"It's you, Lee!" Morrow exclaimed. "I'm glad to see you!"

"Same here, Bill!" Lee returned.

They pumped hands heartily.

"Go on in," Morrow told him. "I'll see you later."

He didn't feel called on to shake hands with Tiny, Dex, Top, and Ryan, with whom he was much better acquainted. "I want a word with you boys," he said. "Step out into the yard."

At the corner of the building three glowing cigarette ends punctured the darkness. Tiny glanced that way and identified the smokers: Duke Rucker, Dent, and Morell.

Morrow made sure he was beyond earshot of anyone before he stopped.

"What's the idea?" Tiny demanded.

"Some of us ain't popular here this evenin'," Bill answered.

"Rucker and those two over there?" Top put in.

"Yeh — and Stash. Stash in particular. It's the trouble he started with Lafoon that's responsible. These folks around the Springs regard cuttin' a man's wire without cause as a purty serious offense."

"I don't wonder," Tiny said thinly. "That's the way we used to regard it . . . Been any trouble so far?"

"Not yet. Some of my boys are inside and they seem to get along all right. The girls refused to dance with your friends over there, and Stash has been gettin' the cold shoulder from everybody."

"You talked to Stash?" Tiny inquired.

"Not yet. I sent in word for him to come out when this waltz is over. I been hearing things for a week. When Jim dropped in the other day I told him what the talk was around Deep Springs. I figgered things might git out of hand here this evenin'."

"Why not let Stash and those gents over there do the worryin' about it?" Joe Ryan asked. He jerked his head in the direction of Rucker and his companions. Joe never had much to say, but that little was usually to the point. "They seem to be the ones Lafoon's put his finger on."

Morrow nodded. "Ben accuses 'em by name. He says he can prove it was them. He's convinced Charlie Edwards and some other big independent owners."

"That lets us out, Bill," Tiny interjected. He was anxious to get on the floor and dance.

"No," the Deep Springs foreman demurred, "it don't let anybody out, Tiny. A thing like this starts, and there's no tellin' where it'll end. We're all B C, ain't we? We can be dragged into this trouble. I aim to stop it if I can. That's why I want to talk to Stash . . . Here he comes now."

Morrow had his say. Stash resented it hotly. He had come to the dance with a chip on his shoulder. Though the hostility directed his way had been brushed aside contemptuously, it had begun to eat into him. It did not improve his composure to see Kit's eyes light up when

82

she caught sight of Lee; and to have her inform him that his brother was there to claim the dance she had promised put a strain on it that was almost greater than it could bear. Bill's challenging remarks, figuratively speaking, supplied the straw that broke the camel's back.

"Nobody asked you for your advice," Stash snarled, relieved to have found someone on whom he could vent his spleen. "If Ben Lafoon's got a bone to pick with me, it's none of your business; and it don't concern Charlie Edwards or any of this bunch around here!"

Morrow refused to back down. "That's not the way they see it," he said flatly. "It's well known that B C has been tryin' to buy Tumble L for a long time. The ruckus you started looks like the heat was bein' put on Lafoon and he was goin' to be made to sell whether he wanted to or not. In other words, you ain't kiddin' nobody, Stash. If grabbin' range is the course B C is goin' to take, someone's goin' to be next, after Lafoon's pushed out. That's what this Deep Springs crowd is saying, and it's got 'em riled."

"Let them think what they please!" Stash whipped out defiantly. "They can put on the ice for me, but they won't start nothing!"

"I don't expect they will," said Bill. "I ain't so sure you won't."

"Maybe I will at that!" Stash boasted.

"If you do — just be sure you know who you're speakin' for."

Stash's eyes glittered murderously. "What do you mean?"

"That you won't be speakin' for me and my crew. I've got to get along with these folks."

Stash rocked with fury. "You're working for my old man, Morrow. Don't forget it."

Bill shook his head. "Your father's name is on the checks I get, but I'm workin' for Jim Brett. I take my orders from him and no one else."

Stash flicked a glance at Tiny, Top, Ryan, and Ferris. He didn't have to ask where they stood. "I'll see about that!" he blazed.

Duke Rucker called him over as he neared the door.

"There's no fun here for us," he complained. "We figger we might as well head for the ranch."

"You stick around!" Stash rifled back. Here were four men on whom he could depend, and he intended to have them handy.

Lee whirled past the window with Kit in his arms. Rucker shot a quick glance at the big man to see how he was taking it. Stash was white around the lips.

"We seem to be takin' it on the chin in every direction tonight," Duke remarked pointedly.

"So what?" was the surly response. "Our night will come. We can wait; I told you we'd have to."

"We been waitin'," Duke reminded him.

"Well, you won't have to wait much longer!" Stash rapped.

CHAPTER
SEVEN

Brother Against Brother

It had not taxed Kit Mosby's sense of perception to realize that something was amiss. She had caught the first hint of it even before she entered the schoolhouse. Johnnie Edwards, Vangie's brother, stood on the steps. He spoke to her, but he had no greeting for Stash. The cut was so deliberate that she couldn't help being aware of it. When they stepped inside more of the same treatment was directed at Stash.

"It's nothing," he said when she asked for an explanation. "It's just a little range trouble. You wouldn't understand it, Kit. Don't worry about it."

She found it a decidedly unsatisfactory answer, and she lost no time getting to Vangie with her question. She quickly had the whole story. Vangie was full of it.

"I suppose Stash was right in saying you wouldn't understand it, Kit. I imagine breaking through a fence and trespassing isn't regarded as much of an offense back East; it's different here. The two forbidden things in this country are rustling and cutting a man's wire. We intend to let him know exactly how we feel about it. Just because he's Stash Cameron he seems to think he can do as he pleases."

She told Kit not to feel embarrassed, that she would find herself as popular as ever. It was an awkward situation, however, and with Lee's arrival a new and more personal difficulty arose. Though Kit was happy to see him, she couldn't help telling herself that she might better not have come. And yet when she felt his strong arms about her, as they glided over the floor, her doubts and misgivings faded.

To make room for the dancing the desks had been carried outside and the benches arranged along the walls. Every seat was occupied.

Kit noticed the friendly nods Charlie Edwards and half a dozen oldsters gave Lee. Among the dancers were a number of young men who, like him, had learned their three R's in this very schoolhouse. They greeted him familiarly and appeared glad to see him again. The lingering, admiring glances of Vangie and the other girls left no doubt of their attitude.

"Everyone seems glad to see you," she said. "Evidently you're not included in the grudge they've got against Stash. When he made the date with me he must have known how he was likely to be received. He might have said something."

"I don't suppose he gave it any thought," Lee replied. He didn't think anything of the sort; he felt that her annoyance was justified; but he was unwilling to exploit it to his own advantage. "This trouble with Lafoon happened before I got home, so there's no reason for anyone to hold me responsible for it. I wouldn't let it distress me if I were you. If anything comes of it, it won't be here." He gazed at her fondly. "You're very lovely tonight, Kit."

His arm tightened about her waist, and he held his breath as he felt her respond to its pressure. There was enchantment in her eyes, in the long curve of her lips. Having her so close, her breath, clean and fresh as mountain laurel just after a rain, touching his cheek, the faint perfume of her hair in his nostrils, had the effect of heady wine on him.

The fiddler and accordionist struck a final note and put down their instruments. Lee danced on and had taken three or four steps before he realized that the music had stopped.

"I was dreaming, I guess," he said with an apologetic smile. "Don't we get an encore?"

"They've given us two already," Kit reminded him. "You waltz divinely, Lee. Who knows, we might win the prize for the best couple seen on the floor this evening."

"Prize?" he queried laughingly. "If I'd known there was to be a prize, I'd have put in a few flourishes. Who are the judges?"

"Mr. Comerford, Vangie's father, and that little man seated next to him."

"Pete Hoffman," Lee said after glancing across the room. "You will save another dance for me, Kit?"

Her blue eyes met his for a moment. "You think you'll be able to tear yourself away from Vangie and Rose Comerford? They're just waiting to grab you."

She took his arm, but Lee wasn't in any hurry to escort her to the benches where Stash was waiting to claim her. His brother's annoyance was unmistakable as he watched them.

"You haven't answered me, Kit," said Lee.

"I know," she murmured. "I came with Stash. You understand."

"That doesn't mean he's got you fenced off, does it?" Lee asked.

"No, I've never given him any reason to think so." Her lips pressed together resolutely. It wasn't a trifling decision he was asking her to make. She sensed that it would carry far beyond tonight. "The first waltz after the refreshments are served, Lee," she said.

He nodded, and it was answer enough.

It was the custom at all Deep Springs dances to have every fourth number a square dance. When the first one was called, it presented a problem that Vangie and the girls who had arranged the affair had not foreseen. They had refused to give Stash a waltz or a two-step, but when he and Kit took their places in one of the sets for the square dance the girls didn't know what to do.

They held a hasty conference. "We'll just have to swing partners with him and make the best of it," Vangie decided for them. "We don't want to embarrass Kit to death. But we can let him know how we feel about it."

Tiny Duprez was in the set and he tried manfully to gloss over the delay with his clowning. The music struck up, and old Corry, the fiddler, began calling the numbers.

The evening wore on without any further unpleasantness. But beneath the high spirits and gaiety of the crowd there was no relenting toward Stash.

"He deserves all he's getting, and more," Vangie told Lee as they tripped through a lively two-step. "But I feel sorry for Kit. She could have had such a good time tonight."

Lee frowned and refused to comment; he didn't care to discuss Kit and his brother with anyone. But Vangie was not to be repressed.

"Has he led you to believe that he means anything to her?" she demanded with her usual bluntness.

"What a question!" Lee gave her a reproving glance that was only half in fun. "I swear you're the same impudent little brat you used to be . . . Why put anything like that up to me?"

"Humph!" Vangie retorted. "I'm not blind; I've got eyes. You give yourself away every time you look at her. Your father has done so much for the Mosbys that Kit felt the least she could do in return was accept Stash's attentions. Don't let him tell you any different."

Lee spun her around dizzily.

"I ought to box your ears for your tattling," he said. Actually he wanted to hug her.

When the music stopped, the accordionist struck a long chord. It was the signal for Charlie Edwards, a round little man, to walk to the center of the floor and announce that there would be an intermission for refreshments.

Though Vangie had come to the dance with Arvid Lindstrom, she invited Lee to share her basket.

"There's enough for three," she said. "I'm sure Arvie won't mind."

The salads and cakes that came from the Edwards kitchen had long been famous. Lee pronounced them as excellent as ever.

His glance strayed across the room to where Kit sat with Stash. Their eyes met briefly, and she smiled. She had a fine, sensitive face, he told himself. The great pride that was in her spoke in everything she did.

Later, when Lee came for his waltz, Stash relinquished Kit to him without a word; but the expression on his rocky face spoke eloquently for him and left no doubt of how he felt about it.

Though he knew he was storing up trouble for himself, Lee did not let it disturb him. Whatever the price for tonight, he was prepared to pay it.

Gliding over the floor with Kit, he found her markedly constrained.

"I know it's been a trying situation for you," he told her. "Please don't take it too seriously. Stash and I have always been at odds. This is nothing new."

"I wish I could dismiss it that easily," she said. "I hope you don't quarrel when you get home. I couldn't forgive myself."

A look crossed Lee's face that left it strong and determined. "I've always given in to him, but there's a line beyond which I won't be pushed."

"I'm afraid for you, Lee," she murmured tensely.

"Don't worry," he said; "I can look out for myself."

Applause began to greet them as they circled around the room. They were a graceful couple, with Kit seeming to anticipate every movement Lee made.

They noticed that some of the other dancers were leaving the floor, and when they turned they saw that the judges were signaling one couple after another to step aside, until only two were left.

"Well!" Lee exclaimed. "It's going to be Johnnie Edwards and Rose or us for the prize!"

To mounting applause, they danced on, doing their best not to appear self-conscious. Without question the majority of the crowd favored them. On the other hand, Rose's and Johnnie's fathers were judging the dancing.

"They can't decide against their very own," said Kit. "I almost wish Rose and Johnnie would win."

"I don't!" Lee objected. "I want you to have the prize. If anyone but Dan Comerford and Charlie Edwards were picking the winner, I'd expect to run second. But they'll call it about as they see it."

The three judges were cowmen and they could have appraised a steer or a piece of range without fear of being wrong. But they knew little or nothing about the fine points of dancing the waltz. That being so, they prudently accepted the verdict of the crowd. After they had conferred briefly, Charlie Edwards raised his hand and announced that Kit and Lee were the winners. He presented the prize, ten dollars in gold, to Kit.

The crowd cheered, and everyone seemed pleased except Stash. For him it only added insult to ignominy.

It was after two before the dance broke up. Lee saw Stash drive off with Kit. Immediately thereafter Rucker and his friends climbed into the saddle and turned their broncs in the direction of Grass Valley.

Lee was walking across the yard with Ryan, Dex, and Top — Tiny was still inside saying his good-bys — when Bill Morrow hailed him. During the course of the evening they had had a lengthy talk.

"We got through this affair without a showdown after all," Bill observed. "But that doesn't mean there won't be one, Lee. It's strictly up to Stash. He left here with blood in his eye. When he flies off the handle there's no tellin' what he'll do. If he'll listen to you at all, try to get him to go slow."

"It would be a waste of breath for me to say anything to him, Bill; he wouldn't listen." Lee shook his head grimly. "I can't get along with him; and I'm through trying. I know tonight was the finish."

Morrow nodded. "Reckon I understand what you mean. It's a terrible thing to see a couple brothers lined up against each other. It'll be hard on your folks. If it's to be an eye for an eye between the two of you, trot your fight out into the open and make it clear where you stand. That'll be better than snipin' back and forth and tryin' to cover up your differences. I'm sure that's what Jim Brett would advise."

Though it was late when Lee got back to the ranch, he had no thought of going to bed. The men turned in and the house grew quiet again as he sat in his makeshift laboratory, trying to read. His thoughts kept straying, and he finally put down his book. There wasn't any doubt in his mind about the mood Stash would be in when he got home.

"If he barges in here looking for trouble, he'll find me ready for him," Lee promised himself.

Daylight was just breaking when Stash drove into the yard. He didn't bother to unhitch the team; he couldn't get into the house quickly enough. Lee heard him come stamping through the dining-room. A moment later he filled the doorway.

Stash had fared badly with Kit on the drive back to the station. She had not only let him know that he was completely out of favor with her but had told him in unmistakable terms that she could not accept any further attention from him. He had promptly charged it up to Lee's account, and as he turned north across the Painted Meadows for Grass Valley his wrath had swelled with every mile he put behind him.

"I'll fix you!" he snarled. "I warned you not to get in my way."

He lunged into the room and with a swipe of his hand swept the glass jars off the table. They hit the floor with a shivery crash and broke into a hundred pieces. It seemed to whet his appetite for destruction. The microscope caught his eye, and he snatched it up and hurled it across the room.

Lee had leaped to his feet. When he saw his treasured microscope go sailing through the air all restraint left him. He flung himself at Stash and drove his fist into the hate-contorted face.

It drove Stash back, but it didn't hurt him. He fancied himself as a rough-and-tumble fighter; this was exactly what he wanted. He wasn't fast; he was too big for that. But there was dynamite in his right hand. He started it at his knees and it was whistling when it lashed out.

Lee saw it coming and avoided it. Stepping in, he hit Stash again, a solid, bone-crunching smash on the jaw that lifted the big fellow to his toes. This time it hurt. While he was off balance, with his guard down, Lee hit him a third time. That blow knocked Stash against the table, which went over with him. Somehow he saved himself from going down.

The house was violently awake by now. Tiny and half a dozen more crowded into the doorway. Others ran outside to peer through the windows.

Stash stood there, his chest heaving with his deep, noisy breathing. Blood trickled from his mouth and spilled over his deeply cleft chin. The fight was not going as he had expected; he should have had Lee on the floor by now, helpless.

He saw that Lee was waiting for him to rush in. Ten feet separated them. Stash lowered his head and catapulted himself forward, covering the distance in that leap. His arms were wide and low. He was in position to bring up one or both and try to reach Lee's chin. But that was not his intention; he was being cunning now. His diving rush carried them to the wall, their bodies crashing into it with a sickening thud. The house trembled under the impact, and above them the cracked plaster was jarred loose and a jagged piece fell to the floor and crumbled to dust.

Lee slashed at the face, his knuckles cutting across Stash's mouth and leaving a red smear. The big fellow took the blow. He had Lee's knees pinioned together, and that was what he wanted. He pulled him forward, took his legs out from under him, and had him on the floor. To make sure that Lee would not get away, he straddled him. Methodically, then, he began to batter him into unconsciousness.

In the doorway a groan was wrung out of Tiny. It seemed that the end was in sight; Lee was trapped, unable to strike back. Tiny knew there was nothing he could do. No one would interfere or try to stop this fight. The silly code that ruled their lives guaranteed that.

Lee's brain reeled as Stash's fists thudded into his upturned face. It was like a woodsman felling a tree with a dull ax. Desperation began to drive him. He knew he had to break free quickly or not at all. He reached out with his hands, trying to find something that would give him the leverage to throw Stash off. All he could touch was a handful of powdered plaster. Even that was something. He wrapped a leg around one of Stash's legs and threw the powdered dust into the big fellow's face. Momentarily blinded, Stash dug at his eyes.

That second's advantage was all Lee needed. With a heave that had all of his waning strength behind it, he bowled Stash over and rolled free. He found the overturned table and used it as a ladder to pull himself to his feet.

Stash got up, his face smeared with dust and blood. He wiped it with his sleeve and set himself for another rush.

Lee kept the table between them. He felt his head clearing and strength coming back to him. Stash began to stalk him. Round and round they went. In his eagerness Stash got tangled up with the table. Lee caught him with left and right, long, slashing blows that shook Stash to his heels. Lee told himself that that was the way to whip him; dart in, punish him, and get away before Stash could set himself for his sledge-hammer blows or pull him down again. With his long arms he had the reach to do it.

Stash sensed that he was being outmaneuvered as the long, punishing shots he was taking began to wear him down. He tried to catch Lee, but the latter was always away in time.

Through the doorway they fought, across the dining-room, and out into the yard. The men formed a ring around them, their faces dark and tense. From Duke Rucker down to old Oddie, the swamper, each one realized that the outcome of the fight must affect him. They knew what the stake was. By and large, the fate of the Brett-Cameron Company was being decided here.

The divided loyalty of the crew stood sharply revealed, the cleavage definite. There never had been any question about where Tiny and half a dozen B C veterans stood; they were Brett men; first and last. There had been some doubt about one or two others. That doubt was gone now; with the chips down, further neutrality impossible, they lined up beside Tiny's faction. Rucker, Bill Dent, Morell, and a fourth man,

Flick Bender, though an uncomfortable minority, did not waver in their allegiance to Stash.

Now that he had room, Lee circled around Stash, hitting him almost at will. It was like a cooper going around a barrel. But though he could rock the big man, he could not knock him down.

"They're tirin' — both of 'em," Tiny muttered. "They can't keep this up much longer."

Stash's right eye was completely closed and his left badly puffed. One of his wild swings caught Lee squarely on the chin and made his knees buckle. Stash was slow in following it up. Lee backed away and managed to keep him off.

Reb Sanders heaved a sigh of relief and licked his dry lips. "When he hit him that time I thought it was curtains," he told Tiny. "Stash put everythin' he had left into it."

The little man nodded. "He's fought himself out. Lee will take him now."

The fight slowed down, but the end was not yet. Both fighters were exhausted. Stash was badly cut up, but Lee had taken a terrific beating too. His face was lumpy and swollen from the punishment he had absorbed, his mouth raw and torn. Whenever Stash gave ground he stalked him, but he no longer rushed in. His arms seemed to have leaden weights in them dragging them down. He half lowered them, conserving what little strength he had left for one final blow.

Stash continued to retreat until he stood at bay in front of the water trough. His long legs were behaving queerly. When Lee saw him tottering he didn't hesitate.

Walking into him, he drove a fist to the jaw. The blow traveled only a few inches, but its impact spread a foolish grin over the big fellow's battered face and all the stiffness went out of him. Down he went, and as he fell his head struck the trough with a sickening thud. He lay there a moment or two and then tried to rise, only to fall back in the dust, not a muscle moving.

The fight was over.

Lee had to spread his own legs wide to keep himself erect. He looked down at Stash, and there was no mercy in his heart; he had suffered too often and too long at his hands.

No one moved. Lee's glance located Duke. "You're his man, Rucker; slosh a bucketful of water in his face."

The cold water revived Stash, but he was still completely helpless. Rucker and Bill Dent picked him up and carried him into the house.

Tiny and Reb tried to give Lee a hand. He waved them off and doused his head in the trough, after which he knelt there steadying himself.

"You put him away, Lee," said Tiny. He spoke pridefully. "I didn't think you could do it."

Lee shook his head. "I don't know whether I could have finished him or not. He struck his head on the trough."

"He was well licked," Tiny insisted. "This may be just what was needed to clear things up between the two of you. At least you boys know where you stand now. I don't say it's the end of your trouble."

"It's only the beginning," Lee muttered prophetically. "You can't make a friend out of a mad dog."

He got up and walked to the house. The laboratory was a wreck. He found the microscope. The barrel was dented and bent, the illuminating mirror broken. The lenses were intact.

"Stash shouldn't have done that," he said soberly. "I'll never forget that he did."

He undressed and bathed his face, doing what he could to ease its ache. The gun he had bought on Brett's advice hung on the wall. It caught his eye. He walked over and pulled it from the holster and slipped it under his pillow. That "accidental" shot in Powder City that had come so close to killing him still needed to be explained. Brett had warned him against someone. Could it have been Stash? The question asked itself. It had to be answered.

Yes, it was Stash!

The thought whipped through Lee's brain with that certainty which brooks no denial. He was suddenly as sure of it as that it was morning. Who else but Stash was interested in having him out of the way? Certainly not Sixto Guerra.

How right Tiny was in saying we know where we stand now! Lee shook his head over it. He thought of Kit. She stood between them, overshadowing all else and quite apart from what had been in Stash's mind that morning in Powder City.

Lee didn't draw away from what he saw in his mind's eye. *It will get to guns. Nothing else will settle the trouble between us!*

CHAPTER
EIGHT

Bushwhacked

The calf shipping always brought at least fifty Brett-Cameron cowboys to town. They were there for the double purpose of attending to the shipping and driving to the ranches whatever stock the company bought in the open market. The arrival of these "feeders" and the shipping of the calves were so timed that there was seldom a delay of more than a day or two.

Though all this activity fell far short of the busy ten days every fall when B C put its beef cut aboard the cars — when Brett-Cameron descended on Powder City in full strength and threatened to take the town apart — it never failed to brew some excitement.

Deep Springs was the first outfit to arrive. Grass Valley got in a few hours later. Stash's face still bore the marks of his battle with Lee. He knew he would be questioned. Rucker realized it too.

Contrary to his usual policy, Stash had brought Duke and his cronies to town with him and left Reb Sanders to straw boss the ranch. Lee had wondered about it and found no explanation.

100

"What you goin' to tell them, Stash?" Duke asked. "You can't deny you had a fight. The more you try to cover it up, the more talk there'll be. Brett will hear about it in a hurry."

"Let him," Stash growled. "I'm through worrying about Jim Brett. He'll have his hands full before he's much older!"

Brett was at the pens, superintending the shipping. He couldn't have escaped hearing about the fight if he had tried. He had nothing to say, but he was pleased to learn that Lee had done better than hold his own.

Jim wasn't the only one on hand to hear what the men had to say; Old Stony, Morgan Cameron's man Friday, was there, sent down expressly to see and hear what he could and report back to the bank. What he learned sent him hurrying into town.

Kit Mosby had ridden into Powder City late in the morning, the errand that brought her only an excuse for her coming. She went directly to the bank, ostensibly just to cash a check. Morg always called her into his private office and had her sit down for a few minutes. She intended that he should this morning. Over the week-end she had found it impossible to tear her thoughts away from what might have happened at Grass Valley. She knew Stash had reached town; she had seen him pass the station at breakfast time. Certainly if there was any news his father would have it.

That she would have any difficulty worming it out of him had not occurred to her, and yet, when she found herself alone with him, a strange embarrassment seized her and she spoke of anything but what was on her mind.

Unknown to her, Morgan Cameron felt equally constrained. He was fully acquainted with every incident that had occurred at the Deep Springs dance, but he did not permit any hint of it to creep in his conversation.

Meanwhile Old Stony cooled his heels outside. When he saw Kit leave he shook his balding head soberly. "By gum," he muttered, "she's worth fightin' fer."

"Well, what is it?" Morg snapped. He knew Stony so well that it needed only a glance to tell him the little man had something of interest to report.

Stony was not to be hurried. He pulled a chair up to the desk and sat down. They understood each other, those two, and there were no secrets between them.

"They fought, Morgan, jest as yuh figgered they would. Stash got back to the ranch, come daylight. He started slammin' things around and Lee waded into him. It began in the house, but it wa'n't big enough for 'em and they finished it up out in the yard. It musta been somethin' to see!"

Morg shook his head. "I know it," he growled. "I was sure they'd go to it. How bad a beating did Lee take?"

"Huh!" Stony snorted. "He whipped the daylights outa Stash!"

"No!"

"Wal, he did. He says it was a standoff because Stash hit his head on the water trough when he went down for the last time, but Tiny says he was fair whipped. It was like that night at Lundy's Ford thirty years ago, when yuh licked Tom McBride and he banged his head agin the bar. He was a beaten man, and everybody knew it. Yuh oughta see Stash. He looks like he stuck his head into a bale of barbed wire."

"He didn't dog it, Stony?"

"No, he jest tangled with a better man. Yuh want me to send him up here?"

"No. So long as it was a fair fight, I ain't going to mention it to neither of them. A licking was just what Stash needed. It couldn't hurt him, and it may knock some of the meanness out of him."

Though he wanted to be impartial, he was definitely pleased on one count. He had never been able to overcome the suspicion that education softened a man. Here was proof to the contrary.

Stony read his thought. "Yuh don't have to worry about the boy, Morgan; he's a Cameron, sure enough!"

Without prompting he supplied the details of the fight as he had got them from Tiny. Morg pieced them together easily enough. He thought he understood now the meaning of the concern he had read in Kit's eyes. He admired her the more for not having said anything.

"Thank God Mattie ain't home to hear about it," he said gratefully. "It'd upset her for fair."

Mrs. Cameron had expressed the hope that the mineral baths at Eureka springs might help her, and Doc Wilkins had urged Morgan to take her down. It was a kindly deception on his part; he knew the baths wouldn't help Mattie.

Stony got up to leave.

"Did Jim have anything to say to Stash?" Morg inquired. He took it for granted that his partner was well informed as to what had happened at Grass Valley.

"Nothin' personal," Stony answered. "Reckon Jim saw it comin' too."

"I hope he don't say anything," said Morg. "It would be a mistake. Let that young woman who was just in here settle it. If she's got half the sense I think she has, she will."

He was ignoring the fact that more than Kit's favor was responsible for the bad blood between his sons. Old Stony realized it. But he nodded; he never questioned anything Morgan Cameron said.

Brett remained at the shipping-pens throughout the long, busy day, threading his way around the catwalk, watching the work go forward to his satisfaction. Though he encountered Stash several times, he made no reference to the fight. That evening, when he and Morg conferred briefly at the bank, he continued to avoid mentioning the matter. It remained for Morg to bring it up.

"I haven't said anything to Stash, and I don't intend to," Jim told him then. "There's nothing I could say. Lee and Stash will have to work this out in their own way."

"That's my idea," said Morg. "I'm glad you agree with me, Jim. Maybe the two of them will get along better after this."

"Maybe," Brett agreed.

He didn't believe anything of the sort. He knew Stash wasn't built that way. Having cut a sorry figure at the dance and, according to all accounts, having had to play second fiddle to Lee would have been enough in itself to inflame him to some desperate retaliation. To have to appear in Powder City and know that behind his back the town was buzzing with news of the licking his brother had given him was asking him to bear too much.

If I know him, he's all rattler now, Jim said to himself as he walked back to the hotel. *Nothing will be too wild for him to try.*

The feeling was strong in him that what he had foreseen was at hand, not only between the boys but between Morg and himself as well. He didn't know what direction Stash's venom would take. Lee would be its ultimate object. Along the way, however, Brett-Cameron could hardly escape being involved. Stash might choose that course deliberately.

He's already got us in hot water, was Brett's unhappy reflection. *If he can pull off something that'll make it impossible for me and Morg to continue together, he'll most likely try it. That's been his purpose all along.*

When he stepped into the hotel he was surprised to see Stash and the little clique of Grass Valley punchers who accepted his leadership seated together in a corner of the lobby. It was only a few minutes past nine, but he had taken it for granted that Stash had long since made his way down to the resorts under the hill and was by now well liquored. But there he sat, sober as a judge.

105

Jim didn't know what to make of it. His curiosity was aroused, and after exchanging a few words at the desk with the clerk he changed his mind about going upstairs and looked around for someone to sit down with to see what developed.

Marsh Effingham, the sheriff, came in just then. They were old friends. Jim hailed him and they sat down together at one of the street windows.

"Shad figured he might have a busy night with all this B C crowd in town," said Effingham. "Nothin' doin' at all so far. Did your punchers hit the bright lights busted, Jim?"

"I wouldn't know, Marsh, unless you're referring to those boys over there," Brett answered with a smile. "I'm sure it isn't money that's holding Stash back."

"Reckon not," the sheriff agreed. "Morg must have been readin' the riot act to him."

Like Shad Childress, the town marshal, Effingham had worn the law badge for years, being re-elected time after time with little or no opposition, thanks to Morgan Cameron. He was a lanky Texan with a deceptively gentle manner and the dusty look of a rangeman. He had just returned from a long-deferred visit to Texas. He had found the changes great since he had seen his home country before, and he was easily induced to talk about them.

As they sat there Brett stole an occasional glance at Stash. It got to be ten o'clock, and he began to wonder if he and Stash were sitting each other out. A few minutes later, however, the big fellow got to his feet.

"It's after ten," he said, loudly enough for everyone in the lobby to hear. "I'm going to the house and turn in. You boys better hit the blankets too. We got a long day ahead of us."

He nodded to Jim and Effingham on his way out. He had no more than left when Rucker and the others drifted out and turned the corner in the direction of the grassy flat at the northern edge of town where the B C wagons always put up.

"Sounded like that was for your benefit, Jim, soundin' off that he was turnin' in this early," Marsh remarked, an amused twinkle in his eyes. "Goin' to bed his first night in town was never Stash's way. I bet he'll be sneakin' down the line before the night's over."

"Whether he does or not is strictly up to him," said Jim. "I'm not riding herd on him. There's no reason for him to throw dust in my eyes."

This was for Effingham's ears; actually Jim was far from being as uninterested as he professed to be. In his mind there wasn't any doubt that Stash's unexpected conduct had a purpose.

Brett had no Stony Jackman to do his bidding, but he had ways of learning what went on in Powder City. A few minutes after he had said good night to the sheriff he strolled down the street and entered the Crystal Palace Saloon and got Big John Ginty aside. Ginty ran the games of chance in the Crystal Palace. Big John nodded in response to Brett's request.

"Won't be no trouble, Jim," he said. "Drop in tomorrow morning and I'll let you know what I found out."

107

Brett was at the shipping pens early. Stash was there ahead of him working at one of the chutes. About nine o'clock the work was going so well that Brett returned to town and went directly to the saloon. Ginty had just come in.

"They didn't see hide nor hair of him under the hill last night," Big John told him. "I got that straight. I checked on it myself."

"Good enough," said Brett. "There must have been some disappointment along the line, knowing he was in town and not showing up."

"Sure," Big John agreed. "Stash is always a good spender. If he'd just sent his money down, he wouldn't have been missed." Ginty chuckled over his own humor. And then: "I wasn't the only one looking for him; I was in Buck Close's place about midnight and I heard little Sixto Guerra ask Buck if Stash had been in. I wouldn't know what he'd be wanting of him. Whisky sure makes strange friends, Jim."

Brett agreed that it did. Apparently Stash and Guerra had not gotten together. It was something to know, though it gave him no clue to what was afoot. Before he got back to the railroad corrals new questions confronted him. Why hadn't they gotten together? Had Stash decided to play his own game? It seemed altogether unlikely. Certainly he and Guerra had not fallen out. Perhaps Stash was trying to create the impression that they had.

The thought stuck in Brett's mind, but it didn't satisfy him. No, he concluded, *that isn't the answer. If it was, he would have arranged to quarrel publicly with Guerra. That would be better than just staying away from him — unless he's framing an all-around alibi for himself.*

Alibi! The word rushed at Brett. Suddenly the truth dawned on him. Alibi! That was it! It answered every question in his mind. By being seen around the hotel until he turned in for the night, by staying away from liquor, Stash was putting himself in the clear for something; and he was doing the same for Duke Rucker and his other loyal adherents.

That evening was a repetition of the previous one. At an even earlier hour Stash announced he was going home. A few minutes after he left his men followed suit.

Brett sat there and saw them go. There was little doubt in his mind that Stash was meeting Guerra secretly. The calf shipping was over; tomorrow the feeders from New Mexico would be arriving. By evening the allotment for Grass Valley would be moving north across the Painted Meadows toward the ranch. It meant that Stash had very little time in which to complete his plans for whatever he was bent on doing.

Though convinced that something sinister and tragic impended, and wanting to stop it, Jim realized that his hands were tied, that there was little he could do. Certainly he could not accuse Stash to his face of anything that was a complete enigma, nor hope to dissuade him by threats of reprisal.

"Guerra is my best chance," he said to himself. "Maybe I can get a line on what's he's doing."

He thought of Maria. She might know something. For whatever the chance was worth, he decided to take it at once.

Leaving the main street, he crossed the flats toward the river. Lights burned in the front and back rooms of Maria's house. Thinking nothing of it, he approached the front door, intending to walk around the house and go to the kitchen as he always did. He was within a hundred feet of the door when voices reached him. He stopped in his tracks. One of the voices was unmistakable.

It's Stash! was his unvoiced exclamation.

He could only guess at the identity of the other. But that didn't tax his imagination.

The door opened without warning a few moments later, and Stash came out, closely followed by Guerra. The two parted without a word, Sixto taking the path along the river that led back to the resorts under the hill and Stash striking off in the direction of camp.

Brett dropped down behind a clump of sagebrush just in time to avoid being discovered. Stash passed within thirty feet of him without suspecting his presence.

Jim remained where he was, hugging the ground, for several minutes. When the night grew still again he got to his feet guardedly. Stash had almost reached the main street and could be seen silhouetted against the lights.

Obviously it had been at Guerra's suggestion that the two of them had used Maria's house for their

110

rendezvous. Brett found it hard to believe that she had any part in it.

When Guerra put it up to her she just about had to consent, he thought. *If she knows anything, I'll get it out of her.*

He found Maria in the kitchen, ironing. Her recent marriage to Miguel Salazar hadn't changed her economic status to the degree that she no longer needed the few dollars her washing and ironing brought in.

"Mr. Jim!" Maria cried. Her dark, liquid eyes were large with fear. She backed away from the ironing-board and crossed herself unconsciously.

Too late, she mustered a smile and tried to pretend there was nothing amiss. When Brett began to question her she tried to deny that Guerra and Stash had been in her house.

"Don't bother to do that," Jim told her. "I just saw them leave. What were they doing here, Maria?"

"I — I don't know, Mister Jim. *Madre de Dios,* I swear it. Sixto, he say he like to meet a friend here. Miguel, he is not home till Saturday. Mebbe he not like it, but I have to say yes to Sixto. I don't know till tonight that he is meeting that young Cameron in my house."

"What did they talk about, Maria?"

"I don't know," she protested.

"Come now!" Jim was losing all patience with her. "In this house not much can be said in one room that can't be overheard in the other . . . You listened?"

111

"*Si*. Cameron give Sixto some money. I know that. He tell Sixto there be more if everything go all right."

After half an hour of trying Brett was satisfied that he couldn't get anything more out of her.

"I've got to believe you're telling me the truth, Maria, and not holding back on me. They didn't see me. I don't want Guerra to know I was here. Understand?"

"*Si*, Mister Jim. I don't tell him nothing."

There was little sleep for Brett that night. Stash had made his deal; the money had been passed. Two or three days, a week at most, and this treacherous business would reach its grisly climax. That it would prove to be an attempt on Lee's life seemed so likely that Brett could think of nothing else. He didn't propose to sit idly by, doing nothing.

"When Stash pulls out for the valley tomorrow I'll go with him," he decided, "and I'll stick close to him until I know what's in the wind, no matter how long it holds me at the ranch."

Stash wasn't shrewd; sooner or later he would unconsciously drop a hint or careless word that would give his game away.

"That'll be enough for me," Brett grimly assured himself. "I just want to be sure."

He had promised himself once before that he would stop Stash even if he had to kill him to do it. He was only renewing that promise.

The stock train was on the siding when he reached the corrals next morning. Bill Morrow and several other

112

foremen were already on hand to have a look at the cattle.

"The stuff looks better than usual, Jim," said Bill. "But I can't help thinkin' of somethin' Lee said."

"What was that?" Brett snapped.

"All we see is cows; we don't give no thought to the army of killers we bring in with 'em. These critters are packin' a lot of ticks. Turn back the hair and you can see 'em."

"Lee will have an opportunity to prove whether he's right or wrong," was Brett's gruff response. "We'll start unloading this stuff."

In the meantime Stash had arrived. In a few minutes all hands were on the job and the work got under way. The frightened cattle came down the chutes with their tails up and were hard to handle. The men cursed in their exasperation; the foremen shouted their orders to make themselves heard above the din of the bellowing cows. Dust began to rise in clouds. Brett kept on the move around the catwalk, bedlam in his ears, and saw order gradually emerge from confusion.

The morning wore on. It had got to be ten o'clock, and after when Shad Childress, the town marshal, came running down from town.

"Jim! Jim Brett!" he yelled through the dust until he got the latter's attention.

"Jim, I got news for you! Ben Lafoon's been murdered!"

The word swept over the pens and in a minute or two Childress was surrounded by a score of men, eager to hear what he had to say.

"Ben was on his way to town this mornin', drivin' in," Childress got out excitedly. "He got only as far as Dutchman's Crick, four miles from home, when someone shot him. He was stone dead when Neph Gibson found him. Ben had been robbed as well as murdered."

Others talked, but Brett stood there stunned for a moment, not only realizing how mistaken he had been in thinking Lee was to be the target of Stash's treachery but sensing to the full what dire consequences the slaying of Ben Lafoon held for the Brett-Cameron Company.

"Was Ben known to be carrying any amount of money?" he asked at last.

"Not accordin' to Gibson, Jim," Childress answered. "He says Ben had only a few dollars on him."

"That's a hell of note," Stash growled. "The cry will go up that we did it and made it look like robbery to cover up our tracks! It means trouble for B C."

Brett turned on him with eyes that were cold and hostile. Stash shifted about uneasily under their frosty stare.

"It sure does mean trouble for us," Jim rapped, "and I reckon that was the intention."

CHAPTER
NINE

A Pinch of Horsehairs

News of the slaying of Ben Lafoon reached Grass Valley before noon. It caused as big a sensation there as it had in town.

"That's a sure way to go lookin' for trouble," Reb Sanders declared when Lee suggested that the two of them leave for Dutchman's Creek at once. "I don't care who killed Ben, B C is goin' to be suspected of havin' a hand in it. That suspicion is goin' to run like a prairie fire."

"You've named the best reason why we should go," Lee argued. "We can't afford not to; we're perfectly innocent and we've got to act like it. You have a couple horses saddled."

It was a long ride to the Creek. When they arrived they found the sheriff, Neph Gibson, and half of Lafoon's crew, as well as Pete Hoffman, who had been one of the judges at the dance, and several other Deep Springs men there. Effingham had established where the killer had waited for Ben to come along. Thirty feet back in the scrub timber and brush there were fresh horse droppings. The leaves of the aspens had been nipped off at several low-hanging branches by the animal. It had rubbed against a tree trunk as it stood there. The bark bore marks, with horsehairs still lodged in them.

Lafoon's body had already been removed to town. The spot where Gibson had found it, and other details, had been described before, but the sheriff had Gibson go over it again.

"You think Ben was in his rig when he was shot?"

"Course I do!" Neph exclaimed fiercely. "There was blood on the seat. He tumbled out after he was hit. The team went on about a hundred yards and stopped. It was a bushwhack job, and you oughta know it, Marsh! Chances are Ben never saw the skunk that got him. Maybe these gents from Grass Valley can give you some information. Why don't you question 'em?"

It had not waited for this thinly veiled accusation to make Lee and Reb aware of the feeling against them.

"We'll be glad to answer any question we can," Lee spoke up. "One of your men, Pat Sears to name him, passed word of what had happened along to Joe Ryan. Joe brought it to the house. We started for the Creek right away."

"Where's your brother?" Neph demanded.

"Powder City, with most of the crew. I'm sure Marsh will bear me out on that."

Effingham acknowledged it with an affirmative nod.

"You're making it awfully plain, Gibson," Lee continued, "that you think we had a hand in this business. If you've got any reason for thinking so, let's hear it."

116

"Brett-Cameron was after Ben's ranch. It'll have to be sold now. That's reason enough for me!" Neph was too angry to have much regard for what he said. "If B C didn't kill him, who did?"

"It's my job to find out," Effingham rapped. "You ain't conductin' this investigation, Neph. If there's any questions to be asked, I'll ask them. Ben Lafoon wasn't easy to get along with. For all you know, this may have been an old grudge that someone took this way of squarin'."

"That's hogwash and you can't make me swallow it!" Gibson flared violently. "This was no grudge killin'; a gent with a grudge to square don't stop to lift a few dollars and a dead man's watch! I'm tellin' you, Marsh, you better fergit how much you owe Morg Cameron and git to the bottom of this!"

The inference that Morgan Cameron owned him and would be protected, no matter what the investigation developed, came close to being too much for Effingham. The glance he leveled at Gibson was cold and steely.

"I know you're excited and have reason to be, Neph, but don't go too far. Let me get the evidence to convict, and I'll pin this killin' where it belongs."

Gibson was ready with another angry retort, but little Pete Hoffman cut him off.

"Let it go at that, Neph," he advised. "Wranglin' with Effingham won't get us anywhere. We know what we think. The whole thing stinks to heaven. Whether the law does anythin' about it or not, we ain't forgettin what happened here. And we won't let Brett-Cameron forget about it either. They've asked for what they're goin' to get."

"That's war talk, Pete," Effingham warned. "You better take it easy."

"You'll find it's more'n talk!" the little man returned hotly. "We'll have Charlie Edwards, Comerford, and every outfit around the Springs with us to a man!"

He and the other Deep Springs men drew aside with Lafoon's crew. After conferring for a minute or two, they mounted and rode off.

Effingham shook his head as he watched them go. To Lee he said, "They've got this all settled in their minds and they won't be talked out of it. It looks like trouble, for sure. I'd advise you to go back to Grass Valley and sit tight till you know what's what. I'm goin' up the creek and see if I can't follow the trail of the gent who shot Ben."

"If you find yourself near the ranch, drop in," Lee invited as they parted.

He and Reb walked over to their broncs as the sheriff disappeared up the creek bottom. Before mounting, Lee extracted seven or eight horsehairs from the bark of the aspen against which the killer's horse had rubbed.

"What's that for?" Reb asked as he saw him place the bits of hair in his metal matchbox.

Lee shrugged. "Nothing important. Just a hunch that they might tell me something when I put them under the microscope."

Reb frowned. "Reckon I'm too ignorant to git that," he declared. "I always figgered horsehair was horsehair, no matter how much you looked at it."

118

He glanced back over his shoulder as they headed north, taking a last look at the crossing.

"I reckon Ben's driven over that road ten thousand times since he hit this country," he mused aloud. "I don't suppose he ever figgered anyone was out to nail him. Cold-blooded murder, that's what it was, and no old grudge killin' either. It's goin' to make things tough for us. Bein' innocent ain't enough; we got to prove it. Thank God, Stash can account for his whereabouts. It ought to put him in the clear."

This suspicion against his brother tightened Lee's mouth. Without glancing at Reb, he said, "Why do you say 'ought to'?"

"It could have been a hired job." Reb was being careful about his answer. "There'll be plenty who'll claim that's what it was. They'll say Jim and your old man was in on it too. It don't make sense; B C don't need Ben's range bad enough to git it that way. But it'll be said, and you know it."

"Undoubtedly," Lee muttered.

They fell silent as they rode along. Try as he would, Lee could not shake off the feeling that his brother was involved. He told himself it was only because he and Stash were so down on each other that he entertained such thoughts.

I'm making the same mistake Gibson and Hoffman are making — leaping to conclusions without having anything to go on, he meditated grimly. I haven't any facts — no evidence, nothing. If I've got any sense, I'll give him the benefit of the doubt until I know otherwise.

It took only the briefest observation of the contents of his matchbox to reward him with one significant bit of information. How important it might prove to be remained a question. He decided to keep the knowledge to himself until he could talk with Jim Brett.

On the surface the life of the ranch seemed to flow on as usual. Lee was not deceived by it; he could feel the tension in the air. To the exclusion of all else, the conversation of Reb and the other men concerned itself with the slaying of Lafoon. It produced endless speculation as to who had killed him and what his taking off was likely to mean to B C.

In another twenty-four hours, or thereabouts, the steers from New Mexico would be arriving at the ranch. The dipping-trough had to be made ready for its first test. It meant hauling water from the creek, and the men were all afternoon at the job. Then Lee poured in his prepared solution. It had to be thoroughly mixed with the water. That was accomplished by having several of the men ride back and forth in the trough for twenty minutes or more.

"That's enough," he called them. "Nothing to do now but wait for the drive to get in."

Some of the intense eagerness and interest with which he had looked forward to demonstrating the merits of dipping cattle were gone from him; he knew matters of graver importance than Texas fever now faced Brett-Cameron. The situation had changed for him personally, too.

He had only to think of Kit and what her reaction would be to the killing of Ben Lafoon to be filled with an even greater soberness. He took it for granted that it would turn Vangie Edwards and Kit's other Deep Springs friends against him. Undoubtedly they would do their best to swing her over to their side.

No, she's got too much sense to be swayed by their talk, he told himself, his eyes narrow and bleak. *No matter what comes up between now and Sunday, I'll ride down to the station; I've got to see her. I know I'm not wrong about Kit. She won't let this trouble come between us.*

Reb noticed Lee's moodiness and at supper he said, "You git your chance tomorrow to prove what the dippin' will do. I figgered you'd be a little more steamed up about it than you are. I know Jim and your old man wouldn't have shelled out the money for you to build the tank if you hadn't made some big claims for what it'd do. You ain't pullin' in your horns now, Lee?"

"Not a bit. It won't be the last tank that'll be built in this country. If Stash shows up with only four or five hundred head, we'll run them through in a few hours. After that it'll be safe to turn them out wherever he pleases."

It was the following noon before Dex Ferris dashed up to the house with word that the drive was in sight.

"Brett's trailin' along with 'em," Dex added. "I could see his rig back in the dust."

Jim's coming was unexpected. Lee surmised that it was occasioned by what had happened at Dutchman's Creek. He was about to tell Reb that they'd get mounted and ride out to meet the drive when he saw that Stash had come on ahead. When he rode up to Lee, Stash didn't get down.

"How do you want to handle this stuff?" he demanded, his old surliness as much in evidence as ever. "There's an even four hundred head."

"Can you hold them out on the flat where the old corral used to stand?"

"Well, of course."

"Do it that way, then," Lee told him: "We'll take six head at a time on this end and shoot them through. We can be finished by three o'clock. This bunch must be a little leg-weary, so it won't drift far. You can move them out tomorrow."

Stash turned back at once. Not a word was said about the killing of Lafoon.

Brett drove into the yard a few minutes later and put up his team at the rack. He was his usual taciturn self. No word of what had happened at Dutchman's Creek came from him. He asked how the dipping was to be conducted and was satisfied with what Lee told him. When the first bunch was hazed into the trough he was there to watch the operation.

The cows rebelled when they got their first sniff of the stinking brown bath in the troughlike tank. Reb and the others went at them with coiled ropes and sharp tempers, and the stock had no choice but to flounder through.

It went better with the next bunch. Lee saw a cow that had its ribs showing, its eyes lusterless. He ordered Reb to drop his loop on it, and with two men holding the animal he picked off a score of ticks and dropped them in a glass-covered dish.

"What was that for?" Brett asked when Lee passed him.

"I can pretty well tell how old these ticks are — especially the females. I'm going up to the house. I'll be back in a few minutes."

The microscope told him what he wanted to know. When he returned to the tank and Brett, he couldn't conceal his elation.

"We're in time, Uncle Jim! The female ticks are swelling up with blood and just about ready to drop off. We'll make a clean sweep of them this afternoon."

The job took longer than expected. No one had eaten since early morning. When the men sat down at five o'clock for a combination dinner and supper they were grumbling among themselves. Hot food mended their injured feelings, and before they had finished they were plying Tiny and the others fresh from Powder City with questions about the murder.

Nothing was said that told Lee more than he already knew. What Stash had to say only echoed what little Tiny and the others were able to supply.

"I hoped you would be able to tell us something, Stash," said Lee. "Reb and I rode down to the crossing yesterday morning. Seems we know more about the murder than you."

"Why should I know anything about it?" Stash flared back indignantly. "I was in the shipping pens all yesterday morning. All I know is the same hearsay talk we all heard. I had a run-in with Lafoon, but it wasn't nothing serious. I suppose some people will try to make something of it. I'm damned if I can think of any reason why I'd want him out of the way . . . Just what did you hear at the crossing?"

It saved Brett from asking that very question.

Lee recounted what had been said the previous morning. It brought Stash to his feet, storming.

"That ain't no more than I expected. Before Neph Gibson goes shooting his mouth off, he better get some facts. If there's any more loose talk out of him, I'll cram it down his throat."

"I don't believe that will stop the talk," Brett said soberly. "But having dug this hole, perhaps the best thing you can do is jump into it."

Stash whirled on him. "What do you mean?"

"Just that I'm taking over here; you've given your last order at Grass Valley."

"Is that so?" Stash retorted with a sneering laugh. "My old man will have something to say about that!"

A break with Brett was what he wanted, but he wasn't prepared to have it come so quickly.

"Your father will have plenty to say about it," Jim agreed. "He's on his way up from town right now. I insisted on his coming as soon as the bank closed. But I can promise you now, Stash, that nothing Morgan may have to say will make me change my stand. I'm not going to have my interest in the company jeopardized any further by you."

The room had grown very still. In his excitement Tiny upset his coffee cup. But no one noticed the interruption. To a man, old hands and new understood that this was the showdown, that having gone this far Brett would never back away from it. As for Lee, he sat in stunned silence, totally in the dark as to what had brought matters to a head with Jim. Certainly the suspicions directed at Stash and the threat of trouble for Brett-Cameron would not have been enough to accomplish it.

It was strange, he thought, that Stash didn't demand an explanation. Instead, his brother flung himself out of the room, cursing, and stamped up the stairs.

His going failed to break the tension that had settled on the dining-room. The crew, especially Duke Rucker and his friends, looked to Brett for some indication of what was to follow.

"In the morning," Jim said, knowing they were waiting for him to speak, "we'll pick up this stuff we brought in today and move it out on our east range. Later in the day I may have something further to say to you. For the present I have nothing to add to what you've heard."

The men were getting to their feet, ready to leave, when someone rode into the yard at a gallop. Lee at first thought it was his father. So did many of the others. To their surprise the man who appeared in the doorway a few seconds later was Marsh Effingham, the sheriff. He jerked a nod at Brett.

"I heard you was here," he said. There was an air of suppressed excitement about him. "Twin Buttes and Deep Springs are in trouble; they can't git through with the stuff they're drivin'."

"Can't get through?" It had brought Jim up sharply. "Why not?"

The question was unnecessary; there could be only one explanation, and he could have supplied it. With only the twitching of a throat muscle betraying his agitation he watched the sheriff walk the width of the room and sit down across the table from him.

"Charlie Edwards is why," said Effingham. "He's standing on his line with his crew and about thirty others. Dan Comerford and Pete Hoffman and 'most any of that Deep Springs crowd you want to name are in the bunch. For years Brett-Cameron has trailed stock to and from its Twin Buttes and Deep Springs ranches across Charlie's range and Dan's, always with their permission, of course. There won't be no more of that, they say. Reckon you know what's behind it, Jim."

"Yes." Brett nodded, more to himself than Marsh. "Yes, I reckon I do." He drummed on the table with his fingers for several moments. "Morrow can turn back to the Dutchman's Creek crossing and go up to the head waters and make the ranch if he has to. Means an extra fifty miles of tough going. I swear I don't know how Holderness can get through to Twin Buttes. There's no short cut."

"He could go through the hills and up the eastern slope of the Big Medicines till he hits Bridgers's Gap," Effingham suggested.

"Two days at best!" Brett shook his head. "It can be done, of course, but I hate to think of trailing beef steers out that way this fall. I've been telling Morg for years that the county ought to lay out a road all the way

126

to the Buttes . . . What did Edwards have to say to you?"

"I ain't seen Charlie," Marsh replied. "I was just leavin' the Double Diamond when Bill Morrow rode by, hurryin' into town to see if Morg could do anythin'. It was Bill who told me I'd find you here. He thought Charlie was bluffin' at first. He's always been friendly with those folks. He tried to call the bluff. There was some shootin'. Nobody got hurt, which was as intended; but those warnin' shots convinced Bill he was up against the real thing. If anybody can talk to 'em it's you, not Morg."

"I don't know, Marsh, I don't know," Brett declared gloomily. "Edwards and his friends are out to make an issue of this. Men won't listen to reason in that frame of mind."

He got up, motioned for the crew to withdraw, and began pacing back and forth. Somehow he was a dejected figure. Effingham noticed it.

"You've faced tougher situations than this, Jim. Where's your fight? What's got into you?"

"When I put up a fight I've got to have a heart for it. I haven't any heart for this trouble. Something will have to be done, of course. I'm expecting Morg here this evening; Bill couldn't have caught him in town. I imagine we'll be seeing both of them. We'll decide what's to be done when they get in . . . You'll have something to eat, won't you?"

Marsh said he would. Brett called Oddie and ordered supper brought in for the sheriff.

Lee had nothing to say, but as he sat at the table with Brett and Effingham, anxious to learn whether the sheriff's investigation had disclosed any clue to the murderer, the opportunity presented itself for him to swing the conversation in that direction.

"I hate to say it, but I'm stopped cold so far," Marsh admitted frankly. "The trail up the crick was easy to follow for a mile or so, and then I lost it completely. If this party had headed toward Powder City he would have been seen. Seems like someone would have spotted him if he had gone the other way, toward Deep Springs. One of Chris Ewing's cowboys thought he saw a man on a sorrel horse skirting the timber in the Slate Hills. But he couldn't be sure. It wouldn't have given me much of a lead at that."

"It wouldn't," Lee agreed. "Sorrels, bays, and chestnuts look pretty much the same at a distance. There's a million of them around. Too bad your man wasn't forking a white horse," he added guilelessly.

"Yeh." Marsh chuckled, not suspecting Lee's purpose. "That would make things considerably easier. I don't suppose there's half a dozen white horses — saddle stock, I mean — in the county."

"Not that many," Brett observed. "There's Doc's mare and the one Deb Taylor's daughter has owned for years. There may be one or two more."

"I know of one, 'way down the river. And there's that ugly bronc Sixto Guerra rides." Marsh thought for a moment. "Reckon that's about the size of it."

Oddie brought in a pot of hot coffee and a platter of fried beef and potatoes.

128

"I'm going in and have another look at my bugs," Lee remarked, getting up. "Come in when you're finished."

It wasn't ticks he had on his mind. The horsehairs he had plucked from the bark of the aspen on Dutchman's Creek were white!

Certainly Doc Wilkins hadn't killed Ben Lafoon, nor had Mary Taylor. That a man on the lower Yellowhorse, a hundred miles away, who probably had never heard of Lafoon, had committed the crime was equally unlikely. It left only Sixto Guerra — Sixto Guerra, the convicted rustler and gunman!

That morning in front of the bank, when Guerra's accidental, or deliberately wild, shot had almost struck him down, was still fresh in Lee's mind. He had thought of it many times, and always with the growing conviction that it had been a premeditated attempt on his life, with Stash its only possible instigator.

No room for doubt remained now, and the slaying of Lafoon was no longer a baffling mystery. It was almost too plain. Only the reasons that had prompted the act remained a bewildering puzzle . . . Stash had hired Guerra to do the job!

"But why?" Lee could only ask it over and over. "Why did he do it? What did he think it was going to get him?"

CHAPTER
TEN

Waiting for the Fireworks

Lee could hear Stash moving around in his room overhead. He listened, trying to catch what his brother was doing. Something thudded against the floor. There was a second thud, and then the squeaking of springs. It was enough to tell him that Stash had pulled off his boots and flung himself down on his bed.

Out in the dining-room Brett and Effingham talked by fits and starts, the rise and fall of their voices reaching him without giving any idea of what they were saying. For over half an hour they sat there. The scraping of chairs came finally, as they got up. Lee could hear them walking to the kitchen door. A few minutes later he looked out the window and saw Marsh riding away.

The sheriff's going surprised him, and when Brett came into the laboratory Lee mentioned it.

"I asked Marsh to leave," Jim told him. "Some things will be said here tonight that I'd prefer he didn't hear. He understood."

He closed the door and shoved a chair in front of it. Not a door in the house boasted lock or key.

"Come over to the window and sit down with me, Lee," he said. "There're some things I've got to say to you — unpleasant things." His voice was as grave as the lines in his weathered face.

"I'm afraid I know what you're going to say, Uncle Jim," Lee told him as they sat down.

Brett shook his head. "I don't believe you do, my boy — not all of it. I fought this thing out with myself all the way up today. When I spoke to your father before I left town I knew the Brett-Cameron Company had reached the end of the trail. That decision was forced on me. What I couldn't decide was whether I should speak frankly to you or remain silent regarding some things of vital importance. You know you've always been the apple of my eye, Lee. If I had had a son, I would have wanted him to be like you. What I have to say doesn't come easy. But I'm sure of this: I'd be failing you if I didn't speak."

"It concerns Stash?" Lee asked, aware of the tightness in his throat.

"Yes. It goes back to the evening before you got home. I was here at Grass Valley when Stony came for him. Your father wanted Stash to be in town to meet you at the train. Stash didn't want you back; he resented your coming. He wasn't going to have you standing in his way, he said. I knew there'd be trouble between you, but I had no idea then how far he meant to go. It didn't take me long to find out; no longer than the next morning. When I met you on the street in Powder City I could have told you what to expect, and I wouldn't have been wide of the mark."

He related Maria's warning against Guerra and Stash, how he had believed at first that he was to be the object of their plotting.

"It was a natural mistake to make," he went on. "It was crystal clear to me that what I had put down as Stash's blundering was actually a deliberate scheme to goad me into breaking with your father and drive me out of the company; but the moment I laid eyes on you I realized you were far more likely to be the target than I. Proof of it came quickly. You must realize by now, Lee, that Guerra and Buck Close staged their phony fight for only one purpose."

"I've been reasonably sure of that for sometime," said Lee. "I've never mentioned it to Stash. Very likely he doesn't even suspect that I ever regarded it as anything but an accident. Maybe I should have nailed him with it. Lafoon might be alive if I had."

Brett gazed at him with an obscure interest. "Then you know, Lee?"

"I think I do. But go on. You've said enough already to explain one thing that's been puzzling me."

Carefully, missing nothing, Brett recounted every move Stash had made during the past day or two in Powder City. He told how he had caught Stash and Guerra at their rendezvous in Maria's house; repeated what Maria had said about Stash giving Guerra money and his saying there would be more if everything went as he wanted it to.

"What was I to think?" Jim asked. "The two of you had fought. By the look of him, he had taken a bad licking. And to get personal, Lee, he had good reason to believe he was running a bad second to you with Kit Mosby. Adding it all up convinced me that another attempt was to be made to rub you out. I was so sure of it that I decided then and there to come up with the drive and stick here, prepared to take whatever steps were necessary to prevent Stash from carrying out his plans. I was wrong. It wasn't you they were after, it was Lafoon. They got him. There's no question about it in my mind. Maybe you feel the little evidence I have doesn't warrant my being so sure."

"I wish I could feel that way," Lee declared tensely. "I'd like to think there is some doubt about it. But I can't. You heard me mention white horses to Effingham. I was after some information. He supplied it."

It was Brett's turn to be surprised. He listened with a still face to the story of the white horsehairs. He waited for Lee to finish before speaking.

"That nails it down, my boy. You were using your head when you picked up those bits of hair. I would never have thought of it . . . What was the puzzle you said I cleared up for you?"

"I couldn't get what Stash was angling for. I do now. What else could he have done that would have been so sure to make trouble for B C? He knew it would drive you out of the organization. First he had to smash Brett-Cameron. He could pick up the pieces then and have things his own way; he knows Dad doesn't want to come back on the range." Lee's tone was thin and bitter. "I suppose he's lying up there right now congratulating himself on his success!"

133

"He'll discover very quickly how badly he's miscalculated a number of things," said Brett. "He needn't expect any consideration from me."

In the gathering twilight Jim gazed across the range he knew so well, and there was pity and regret in his eyes.

"This is going to be hard on Morgan. He's a proud man!"

"Just what are you going to say to Dad?" Lee demanded.

"About Stash?"

"About everything."

"As far as the business goes, I don't propose to drive a hard bargain. I've always said I'd never let go of my half interest in Grass Valley. I'll take this ranch and Deep Springs; he can have the rest. His lawyer and mine can work out the details. As for what is to be said about Stash, that's something for you and me to decide right now, Lee.

"A man can be satisfied in his own mind that he knows such and such is the case, but that doesn't mean he can go into a court of law and prove it. That's the situation in which we find ourselves. We're sure we know who killed Ben Lafoon. We have some evidence to that effect. It isn't strong enough to convict, not with the judge, prosecutor, and jury under pressure to favor the defendant. And they will be under tremendous pressure, Lee; Morgan will move heaven and earth to save Stash, and that means saving Guerra too. Much of what we know will be thrown out as not admissible evidence. Why, even those white horsehairs won't stand up. We can't swear they came from Sixto Guerra's bronc. And yet we know something, and we are forbidden under penalty of law to withhold it."

"Don't make me agree to that!" Lee protested, and not because he felt any trace of pity or forgiveness for his brother. "You talk about Dad being shamed and crushed. What do you think it would do to my mother? It would kill her to have Stash standing trial for murder. It would be too much for her even if he were acquitted. I'm not fooling myself, Uncle Jim; Mother hasn't long to live. I couldn't do this to her."

Brett nodded sympathetically. "I appreciate all that. But there's something else for you to consider. Stash has got to be stopped. If he's left free to pursue his murderous course, you'll be shot down one of these days, just as Lafoon was."

Lee didn't hesitate over his answer. "I'll take my chances on that," he said, his face hard and flat as he spoke. "It won't be as though I didn't know what to expect from him. I figure I can take care of myself."

"No, Lee! You're dealing with a mad dog. I didn't question your courage, but courage never protected any man against a shot in the back!" The old cowman shook his head grimly. "Ben was a brave man by my standards; he didn't have a chance. Stash won't give you a chance. You won't be safe as long as you figure to be in line for anything he wants. I'm not speaking only of the Cameron ranches. When your father passes on he'll leave a fortune to the two of you. Stash knows it. If he can put you out of the way, it'll all be his."

"I've thought of that," Lee declared, his voice toneless. "I'll leave him no reason to worry on that score. If it will spare Mother the agony and disgrace of seeing him exposed for what he is, I'll cut myself off without a dollar of Cameron money. It can be done tonight — if you'll stand by me."

Jim gazed at him aghast. "I don't know what's in your mind. Whatever it is, I'll stand by you. But Lee, think things over carefully before you burn your bridges behind you. What is it you're asking me to do?"

"I want you to give me a job — fit me into something you feel I can handle. That'll take care of everything. It'll turn Dad against me and give Stash what he wants."

"Good Christopher!" Jim burst out incredulously. "You don't know what you're saying, son. There's nothing I'd like better than to have you with me — not as a hired man but as my partner. But you can't slap your father down like that. He'd swear to the day he died that I put you up to it. There must be a better way."

"It's the only way, Uncle Jim. I know how bitter he'll be, but if I can stand up to him and take it without letting him know why it's got to be that way, it'll be the kindest thing I could do."

Night came on. Far to the south, Bill Morrow ate a hasty supper at the Dog Iron ranch and got the loan of a fresh horse. He had been in the saddle all day, but when something needed doing he never let his weariness interfere with getting it done. From what he had learned at Dog Iron, he knew Morg was less than two hours ahead of him, driving the high-stepping team of matched bays of which he often boasted the equal could not be found in that part of Wyoming.

Even allowing for the short cuts a horseman could take, while a team and rig would have to follow the winding road, Bill realized he could hardly overhaul the old man before he reached Grass Valley. That was all right with Bill. Having run into gunfire a dozen miles east of Dutchman's Creek, he wasn't in any doubt as to the seriousness of the situation B C faced, and he intended to be told what he was to do about it by Jim Brett, not by Morg Cameron.

The moon came up to aid him. But though he touched up his bronc with the spurs where the going permitted, his calculations proved correct and he was almost in sight of the Grass Valley house before he saw Morg's rig moving over the road ahead of him.

Morg had heard the ugly suspicions against Stash and Brett-Cameron that had sprung into circulation almost as soon as news of Lafoon's slaying reached Powder City. His innocence of any such conniving himself, and his knowledge that Jim Brett would never have countenanced it, had immediately convinced him that Stash was equally blameless and that it was just one of those vicious, irresponsible attacks that were always being directed at any organization that was strong enough to reach the top of the heap.

He was totally ignorant, however, of the action Charlie Edwards, Comerford, and Pete Hoffman had taken with the active support of other Deep Springs

137

cowmen. The long drive, coming on top of the slanderous talk and the stormy session he had had with Jim that morning, to say nothing of what he feared he would have to face when he reached Grass Valley, had whipped him into a bitterly contentious mood. When he heard what Morrow had to say he exploded.

"Hellsfire, why didn't you go through 'em?" Morg growled. "They'd have scattered like quail if you'd showed 'em you meant business. I've had outfits try to stop me when Brett and I was so near broke we was just one jump ahead of the sheriff. Where do you think we'd be today if we'd turned around with our tails between our legs and let 'em bluff us out? You get back there and drive through tonight! If Edwards wants to go to law about it, let him!"

"It means war, Mr. Cameron." Brett was always just Jim to Morrow, but he had never been able to bring himself to address Morgan Cameron with similar familiarity. "If that's what you want, Holderness and I will try to get through. But if that's to be an order, Jim Brett will have to give it."

To have his authority questioned so openly made Morg wince. Nothing could have shown him more clearly how completely he had lost his grip on Brett-Cameron. A blistering rebuke rose to his lips, only to be withheld as he thought of Jim. He knew their empire of grass and cattle was tottering tonight, that he had to placate him. To go over his head was not the way to do it.

"That's as it should be, and it's perfectly agreeable to me," he declared in quite another tone. "You know I wouldn't do anything, Morrow, till Jim okayed it."

Lights still burned in the bunkhouse when he and Bill rode into the yard. It lacked only an hour of midnight, but the crew was still awake, waiting for what Tiny called the "fireworks" to start.

"I'd sure give a leg to hear this powwow!" he declared as Morg and Bill entered the house. He expressed the feeling of all the others.

All evening they had been so engrossed with what was to come of this meeting of the partners that they were completely off guard. Though they knew trouble was in the saddle and riding a wild horse, it never occurred to them that they were being watched, and had been for several hours.

Tiny Grass Creek flowed along one side of the ranch yard. With a running start a man could leap across it any place; but, as was the case with every creek in the country, a fringe of willows and buckbrush grew along its winding course. Safely hidden behind that screen, six men had bunkhouse and ranch house under close surveillance. The buildings were less than a hundred yards apart. The position the six men held placed them squarely between the two.

They had reached their point of vantage easily enough. Grass Creek flowed into Buckshot Creek just below Lafoon's Tumble L line. They had only to leave their broncs at a safe distance and come up Grass

Creek on foot, with the willows to shield them, to avoid being detected.

They were not at all hazy about what they were there to do. It was nothing less than to take Stash Cameron out of the house, alive if possible, and carry him off to a suitable place where they could put some questions to him. What they did with him after that would depend on what he had to say. They were of an open mind about it, but they were ready to carry out whatever judgment they passed on him.

In Slick Peasant's barroom at Lundy's Ford they had made their plans. All day long they had brooded over the manner of Lafoon's passing. Slick's whisky had clarified the situation to a remarkable degree and left them in no doubt as to what their duty was. Ben had been foully murdered; he had always been a good boss; it was up to them to avenge him.

They had no evidence against Stash. They needed none, they told themselves. Neph Gibson had summed it up for them when he said, "What's evidence? We can put two and two together. A skunk's a skunk, and you don't have to see him to know one's been around!"

From their place of concealment they saw Morg and Bill Morrow arrive.

"That explains it," Neph muttered savagely. "They was expected. That's why them gents ain't asleep."

He and the other Tumble L punchers hadn't been able to understand why lights had continued to burn in both the main house and the crew's quarters. Long before this they had expected to be able to steal into the ranch house, faces masked, and grab Stash. They had counted noses and knew that, aside from him, they would have only Lee and Brett to contend with. They had even located Stash's room. The B C crew didn't figure to interfere, no matter what happened; they were penned up in the bunkhouse and two men could keep them there.

Neph and his cohorts knew Charlie Edwards and Comerford had denied B C a right of way across their range. That Morrow's presence at Grass Valley was for any other purpose than to hold a council of war with the owners of the brand was not open to question in their minds.

"The damn' range hogs are goin' to cook up some more dirty work!" Kize Lafoon ground out. He was distantly related to Ben and the others recognized his right to be bitter. "We'll never git all of 'em together ag'in like this. They'll git together in the dinin'-room. We can creep up to the windows and settle their hash so it'll stay settled!"

Neph said no. He wasn't ready to go that far, though he was sorely tempted. He looked around at the others; he was head man and he let them know it. "Stash is the gent we want. If anybody's got a different idea, he can forgit it! We'll sit tight a while longer."

Kize was not easily silenced. "There's five men in there now," he argued! "We can git in the house all right, but we'll never git by the five of 'em, no matter how long we wait, without having guns shoved in our faces. That old butterball Morg Cameron won't bother us much, but you ain't walkin' over Jim Brett. I don't know 'bout young Lee Cameron. From the little I've seen of him, he's got some guts. When it comes to Morrow, you know he'll put up a fight."

Neph was forced to admit that Bill's presence complicated matters considerably. "Ain't likely Bill will stay the night here," he observed contentiously.

The words were barely off his tongue when Morrow stepped out of the house. The Tumble L riders riveted their attention on him, hoping he was about to leave. The hope was short-lived, however, for Bill yanked the saddle off his bronc and started to lead the animal down to the corral.

Tiny Duprez came to the bunkhouse door and called to him as he passed.

"What's doin', Bill? We ridin' tonight?"

"No, you boys can hit the blanket," Morrow replied. "Jim says that as far as he's concerned no cause will be given for further trouble. He's ridin' back with me in the mornin' to have a talk with Edwards and Comerford. If they won't agree to let us through, we're goin' to swing around their range and get home the best way we can."

Neph and the Tumble L men caught it all. They held their tongues until Bill returned to the house.

"What do you make of that?" Kize Lafoon was quick to ask, the moment the door slammed.

"I dunno," Neph muttered fiercely. "Looks like some of the wind was knocked out of my sails. Sounds as though Jim Brett might have had this whole thing put over on him and didn't know nothin' about it till it was too late to be stopped. Damn me, that's sure one thing

142

Stash Cameron is goin' to clear up for us when we git our hands on him!"

"That ain't goin' to be tonight," one of the other men spoke up. "You heard Morrow say he was stickin' here till mornin'. Jest what are we goin' to do, Neph?"

"We're goin' to git outa here and come back tomorrow night."

"Pull away without even makin' them hit the floor?" Kize demanded incredulously. "We slapped lead into that house once before, and we'll give 'em another taste right now!"

He started to get his gun out of the leather. Neph stopped him.

"You try that again and I'll poke that .45 down your gullet, Kize!" he whipped out threateningly, "You want to make it impossible for us to come back?"

Kize saw he had no one to support him. "Okay," he agreed grudgingly. "Let's git goin'."

In single file they moved down the creek, with Neph bringing up the rear. The evening hadn't gone his way but it had not been a complete failure. He had learned something of interest, even though he couldn't be sure what it meant.

"Somethin' peculiar about the get-together they're havin'," he reflected solemnly. "Morrow got his orders two minutes after he got there. And they was Brett's orders. Jim couldn't have give Morg Cameron even time enough to git his tongue limbered up."

He mulled it over at length, trying to find the correct explanation among the several that offered themselves. The dispatch with which B C's difficulty at Deep

Springs had been disposed of indicated it couldn't have been anything connected with that situation that had brought Morgan Cameron to Grass Valley tonight.

"No, sir," Neph decided. "It was somethin' else brought the old highbinder all the way up from Powder City. He ain't there 'cause he wanted to be."

CHAPTER
ELEVEN

Showdown

Though it was true, Neph's contention that Morgan Cameron was not at Grass Valley tonight because he wanted to be was also a gross understatement. Morg's worst fears had been more than realized as he sat in the battered, smoke-begrimed dining-room and heard Brett deliver his ultimatum, his round face alternately ashen with desperation and purple with rage. He knew the Brett-Cameron Company had breathed its last and he was only there to attend its demise.

His sons sat with him. Morrow had prudently taken himself up the stairs to bed.

"You must have known this morning what you were going to do," Morg whipped out accusingly. "Why didn't you say something in town?"

"I wanted to say it here — where we started. We've come a long way since those days, Morg. But we can skip that; I just want you to know that it was never my wish to have it end this way. But it's too late for talk. We could sit here all night and it wouldn't change my decision in the slightest degree. I want to be more than fair with you; that's why I'm asking only for this ranch and the Deep Springs property. I'll have Henry Warren take care of the legal end of it for me. You can give him a financial statement of cash on hand and the other assets of the firm. Your word will be good enough for me. I want everything handled in as friendly a manner as possible."

"Friendly!" Morg snorted angrily. "Do you think you can do this to me and have anything friendly about it? You know well what folks are going to say when it gets out that we've split up. Right and left they'll be whispering that there must be something to the lying talk that Stash was mixed up in the killing of Ben Lafoon. It ain't what you're asking for that makes me see red. Take Grass Valley and Deep Springs! If you was honest enough to come right out with it, you'd have to admit you believe the rotten stuff they're saying against Stash! That's what is behind this. You don't give a damn what it does to him."

"Stash has made his bed with me and he'll have to lie in it," Jim replied bluntly. "If he doesn't like the ugly talk that's going the rounds, he can blame himself for it. He went out of his way to pick a fight with Lafoon. I used to make excuses for him, that was my mistake. He wasn't blundering, he was crossing me deliberately. For over a year he's had his mind set on forcing me to get out. It's taken him a long time, but he's had his way about it. I hope he's satisfied."

Stash had had very little to say. He felt he could afford to hold in. Even now he scarcely bothered to defend himself. "Think what you please," he said contemptuously. "Because you say a thing is so don't make it so. You ain't God Almighty, Brett." That was all.

146

How simple it had been to bring this thing off the way he wanted it! Stash couldn't help marveling over it. Jim's demands were less than he expected; Twin Buttes and Kelly Creek were almost as profitable as the Grass Valley ranch; Ruby Lake was smaller but, with its unfailing water supply, had always been one of the strongest links in the Brett-Cameron string; the others, Iron Point and Big Coulee, could be developed and would be immensely valuable if the government ever got around to putting in a dam on the upper Yellowhorse. He didn't doubt his ability to weld them together and make them a more important organization than B C ever had been. When he got things moving, new links could be added.

The Tumble L would be put up for sale. He wouldn't let his father do anything about that, Stash decided. Buying the property would be a little too raw. He wanted Ben Lafoon to be forgotten.

Looking ahead, he realized he wouldn't have everything his own way at first; he'd have Lee to contend with. But that wouldn't be for long; he knew how to take care of him. Though it bored him to listen, he held his tongue as Morg argued in vain to get Brett to change his mind.

"Why keep on chewing the fat?" Stash rapped at last, unable to bear any more of the useless wrangling. "Lee and me can take over and run the ranches as good as they've ever been run. If Brett thinks he's got us where the hair is short, he's mistaken!"

Morg turned on him fiercely. "You keep out of this, Stash!" he thundered. "If you'd used your mouth a little less and your head a little more, things might have worked out different! When I want your advice, I'll ask for it."

He focused his attention on Brett again.

"You don't have to pay no heed to what Stash says; this is between you and me, Jim. All I'm asking you to do tonight is hold off for a few days and take time to think things over before we take any final action."

Jim shook his head; he was not to be moved. "It wouldn't change anything, Morg. This is final. There's just one thing I want to say, and that concerns the brand. It'll have to be retired; I'll file for a new brand and you'll have to do likewise. I always took pride in being able to say when the B C brand was put on a cow it would never be vented. But that's what'll have to be done now. It's part of my bargain."

"That's a job of rebranding that'll take all summer!" Stash burst out vehemently.

"It won't take us all summer at Grass Valley and Deep Springs," Jim told him. "If you're going to take charge for your father, you want to do something about your Twin Buttes drive that's stalled on Edwards' line. You heard me tell Morrow I'd go over with him in the morning and see what I can do. I'll be speaking for my own outfit, not for yours. And by the way, there's four men on the ranch who can't work for me. When you leave, take them with you. You know who they are without my naming them."

He pushed back his chair and got to his feet. He looked tired and weary and his drawn face seemed thinner than ever.

148

"I'll bid you good night," he said, turning to the stairs.

"Just a minute, Uncle Jim," Lee spoke up. "You know what I'm going to say but I want you to hear it. Everything that's been said tonight concerns me as much as it does Stash. It's up to me to tell you where I stand, Father."

Morg sucked in his breath with a noisy gasp and his face took on an apoplectic hue. It was as though he had received a premonition of what was coming.

"What do you mean — where you stand?" he demanded indignantly. "You stand with your brother and me. The two of you will have to put a shoulder to the wheel and pull together, and that's how it's got to be. I guarantee you I'll bring Stash down off his high horse. It's a fifty-fifty proposition between you from now on."

"No, Dad, Stash and I are taking different trails after tonight," Lee said firmly. "I'm sorry, but that's the way it's got to be. I'm sticking with Jim."

"*What!*" Morg leaped to his feet, shaking with fury, so utterly beside himself that he couldn't speak for a moment. His blazing eyes fastened on Brett. "This is your rotten work!" he roared. "You put the boy up to this!"

"You're wrong; this is nobody's work," Lee told him. "I thought this out for myself. I didn't want to hurt you, but I realized this was the way it had to be."

It staggered Morg. He had to sit down. "You was always the gentleman in the family; I was so proud of you," he muttered heavily. "I gave you what I never had myself — an education!"

"You've done a lot for me," said Lee. "I'm grateful to you for all of it."

"You sound it!" Stash jerked out caustically. "Go your way. That'll suit me fine."

"I know it will!" Lee retorted, anger boiling up in him too. "You're top dog now; you can throw your weight around as much as you please. But you won't be throwing it at me!"

Morg silenced them. "Things have got to a pretty pass when a man has to face a thing like this at my time of life. I'm telling you, Lee, you'll reconsider, or I'll cut you off without a dollar, so help me."

Lee didn't hesitate over his answer. "That's how it'll have to be, Dad; my decision stands."

"Then get out of my sight!" Morg cried. "Don't ever speak to me again! And that goes for you too, Brett. I'm pulling out of here right now. I wouldn't spend the night under the same roof with either of you. You go upstairs and throw your junk together and put it in my buggy," he told Stash. "You're leaving with me."

"Sure," Stash agreed. He could scarcely believe his good fortune. The whole cake was to be his now. He turned to Brett. "I'll take Bill Dent, Morell, Bender, and Duke with me. You get their time ready. The books are there on the shelf."

He hurried up to his room, anxious to get away before anyone could change his mind. His anxiety on that score was uncalled for. Jim got down the current book covering the business of the ranch and cast up the

150

accounts of the four men. Morg ignored him, sitting hunched over in his chair, angry and defiant but somehow a pathetic figure.

With an effort Lee pulled his eyes away from his father and walked out of the dining-room. He closed his door and turned out the lamp. His father had his faults, but he had always been fond of him.

He's taking it just as hard as I thought he would, he said to himself as he sat down at the window, the clutch of emotion resting heavily on him. *It's tough for me too. Awfully tough. Thank God Mother won't know what to make of it.*

Stash made several trips out to the buggy with his personal belongings. Later Lee heard him going down the yard to rout out Duke Rucker and the others. Jim's familiar light step sounded on the stairs. It left Morg alone.

The urge to have a last word with his father took Lee to the door. But he didn't open it. *It would just make it harder for him,* he decided. *It's better to let it go the way it is.*

Twenty minutes to half an hour passed before he caught the sound of moving horses and the creaking of buggy wheels. Through the darkened window he could see the little cavalcade moving away. Stash was taking his private string of broncs. Duke owned an extra horse, as did Morell. Morg led the way. Stash and the others, their unmounted animals on lead ropes, followed close behind.

Lee watched them until they were no longer visible in the moonlight. Loneliness began to gnaw at him.

151

Knowing sleep was impossible, he left the house and walked for over an hour, trying to get a grip on himself. Weariness finally sent him to bed. It was almost three, and it seemed to him that he had no more than closed his eyes when he heard the cook lighting the breakfast fire in the kitchen.

Brett was in the dining-room when the crew trooped in. He spoke at some length of the changed status of the ranch and the dissolving of the Brett-Cameron Company. Reb Sanders would be the new foreman of Grass Valley, he told them. The record in his little black book said Reb deserved the job. The announcement sat well with the men; Reb was one of their very own, and as they expressed it he had "a head on his shoulders." To Reb it came as a complete surprise.

Tiny yanked him to his feet and told him to say something. The little man felt no resentment at having been passed over.

"Reckon you know I'm obliged to you, Jim," Reb said simply. "I'll try to ramrod this outfit in a way that'll please you."

"I'm sure you will, Reb," Brett told him. "It's going to be a busy summer for all hands, with all the rebranding that'll have to be done. We'll get by all right if we can escape a bad bout with Texas fever. Lee is confident it'll give us little or no trouble at Grass Valley."

"I wish we had that dippin'-tank at Deep Springs," Bill Morrow spoke up. "I know Lee's as right as rain in saying the ticks do somethin' to a cow's blood that turns it to water. Last August, when we were losin' six, seven head of stock a day, I took a healthy-lookin' yearling and put it in a box stall and hand fed it. I scraped off every tick I could find on the critter, but it took sick and died. It was something in the blood — some bug."

"That's exactly what it was," Lee assured him. "The microbe of Texas fever, put into that cow's blood stream by the ticks you picked off, punctured the blood cells. You were too late to do anything, Bill. If you'd destroyed the ticks before they got in their deadly work, your yearling wouldn't have come down sick. We couldn't put in a concrete tank at Deep Springs like the one we have here in time to be of much use this year. We could build something with planks and canvas that would be a satisfactory makeshift. It wouldn't cost much." He was addressing himself to Brett more than to Morrow. "If we do anything it'll have to be done at once; we can't wait till the results at Grass Valley prove what dipping will do."

"I know it," Jim acknowledged. "It isn't the expense that makes me hesitate about telling you to go ahead and do what you can, it's the amount of work we've got in sight. It would call for extra men at Deep Springs. We couldn't supply them from Grass Valley; we're going to be shorthanded here. At this time of the year I don't know where I'd find the type of men I'd care to take on."

"Jim, you'll have men galore stringin' you for a job before the week's out," Morrow declared emphatically. "I mean old Brett-Cameron men. I can name a dozen who won't work for Stash."

153

Bill was delighted over the change that had taken place. Nothing could have pleased him more than to find himself working for Jim Brett.

"Well, we'll see," said Jim. "I won't do anything to wean them away from their present job. But if we can build up to full strength, we'll put in some sort of a dipping-tank at Deep Springs."

Breakfast over, Brett took to the saddle with Lee and Bill and struck out for Dutchman's Creek. They took the road at the crossing and followed it to where it ended at Charlie Edwards's Box E line.

The Deep Springs and Twin Buttes drives had moved back from the fence and stood where they had been held for the night, one to the right of the road, the other to the left. Watching them from across the fence, fully thirty men stood on guard. Half of them had been there continuously since early afternoon of the preceding day. Daylight had brought the others, including Charlie Edwards and his neighboring ranchers, Dan Comerford and Pete Hoffman, back to the line.

Guy Holderness, the Twin Buttes foreman, rode up to the road and stopped Brett. "There's more of them over there than ever," he said, indicating the fence with a jerk of his head. "They're not going to let us through, Jim. What do you want me to do?"

"Stash hasn't showed up yet, eh?"

"I didn't know he was expected," Holderness replied, plainly puzzled.

"He'll be here," said Brett. "You'll have to look to him for your orders, Guy; Twin Buttes is now a

154

Cameron ranch. Bill can explain things to you. Lee and I are going to ride up to the fence."

Edwards, Comerford, and little Pete were coolly hostile as they came up to talk with Brett.

"The first thing I want to say is that there's no longer any Brett-Cameron Company," Jim began. "I'm here this morning representing only myself. Morg and I reached the parting of the ways last night."

He told them as much as he thought they should know. Edwards and his neighbors listened skeptically.

"Sounds to me like a slick trick to pull the wool over our eyes," Hoffman declared bluntly. "If you've split with Cameron, what's his son doing here with you?"

"Go ahead and explain that," Comerford invited, sharing Pete's suspicion.

"Let me answer," Lee interjected. "I'm not foolish enough to think it's any secret that my brother and I have always got into each other's hair. When the break came last night I had my choice of going to work for Stash or staying with Jim. I chose to stick with Jim Brett. And I don't intend to apologize to anyone for my decision or ask any favors because I made it."

Edwards nodded. "That sounds like straight talk to me, which is no less than I'd expect from you, Lee. I can't say the same for your brother. What I don't understand is why Jim waited till Ben was killed before you got a bellyful of Stash. Why was that, Jim?"

"I've had a bellyful of him for a long time," Brett replied thinly. "Several weeks ago I was ready to call it quits and allowed myself to be talked out of it on the strength of his promises to turn over a new leaf. B C wanted to buy Lafoon's range. When he refused to sell, I repeatedly warned Stash not to have any trouble with him. I knew what the talk would be if anything happened that might look as though we were putting pressure on Ben. There was trouble, and immediately you were sure Brett-Cameron was getting ready to squeeze him out."

"If you'd been in our boots, you'd have felt exactly as we did," Edwards insisted. The breaking up of Brett-Cameron invalidated much of the reasoning that had led him and his neighbors to take their present stand, but Edwards wasn't ready to admit it, nor were the others. "We wasn't altogether wrong," he continued. "It's a fact that Ben was murdered."

"Yeh, and what Brett's had to say narrows things down considerable!" Pete Hoffman piped up. "If he's tellin' the truth, and I reckon he is, we got more grounds than ever for suspecting who was responsible for the blastin' Ben got!"

"We ain't accusin' no one — not yet," Edwards, observed cautiously. "If it's okay with Dan and Pete, I'm willin' to let you come through, Jim. But the bars stay up for Stash Cameron."

Comerford and Hoffman nodded their agreement.

"I miss my guess if runnin' his old man's ranches doesn't go to that pup's head," Edwards added. "He just wants to try throwin' his weight around and runnin over other folks's rights, and we'll show him what he's up against."

"Speaking of a man's rights, Charlie," said Brett, "I recognize your right to refuse to let me through. Sooner than have any argument about that, I'd turn my stuff around and drive it home by way of Dutchman's Creek and the hills."

"No, come through," Edwards told him. "Git your stuff movin'."

Brett and Lee swung their broncs and jogged back to the herd.

"They say we can go through, Bill!" Jim called to Morrow. "Let's get going."

They had the cattle moving toward the gate when Stash came pounding up the road. He had Duke Rucker and the other ex-Grass Valley punchers with him. They had spent the night at the Dog Iron, since Ab Hutton, the owner, was always ready to do Morgan Cameron a favor. Stash found Holderness at once, and from the activity that followed Lee saw that Twin Buttes intended to follow them across the line. He mentioned it to Jim.

"They're going to try it," Brett agreed, glancing back. "They'll be stopped, and if they attempt to force their way there'll be a fight."

Once started, the Deep Springs cows poured across the line and moved out on Edwards's range. With their passing three men leaped forward and relocked the gate. The Twin Buttes herd was moving up the road, only two hundred yards away. Stash saw what had happened. He spurred out of the dust and raced up to the gate.

"What's the idea?" he roared. "You just let Brett through. Do you mean to say we don't get the same shake he got?"

"That's the general idea," Edwards informed him. "My range is closed to you, and it stays closed."

Stash didn't ask for an explanation. One was hardly necessary; he knew to the letter what these men were thinking. Beside himself, he whipped up his .45 and put a slug into the lock that shattered it. Half a dozen men had him covered instantly. With cool deliberation Pete Hoffman shot the gun out of his hand, the ricocheting bullet cutting a red furrow up Stash's arm. Rucker and the other three started to rush to his side only to run into a fusillade of shots. The slugs whining about their heads were a convincing argument and turned them back.

The cattle, now without water for almost twenty-four hours and jittery in these strange surroundings, broke in the face of the gunfire and stampeded through the brush, tails up and horns flashing in the morning sunlight. Holderness and his crew went after them, trying to get them turned.

"Pick up your gun and git outa here, you big two-legged sidewinder!" Pete yelped.

Stash examined his arm. The wound was trivial. Taking his time, he retrieved the gun. "I'll remember this," he snarled when he had swung up into the saddle. "Before fall comes I'll be driving through here. You'll use your gate for kindling wood, Edwards."

The threat wasn't as empty as it sounded; there was an idea behind it. Edwards and the Deep Springs men weren't impressed. They had stopped him, and they jeered as he rode away.

Brett and Lee had seen it all.

"I don't know what to make of it," said the latter. "Even a halfwit would have known better than to think he could get away with anything like that. He's lucky to be alive."

"His luck will run out on him," Brett commented sagely. "Give Stash rope enough and he'll hang himself. I didn't intend to go all the way to Deep Springs. But I will. We'll see what we can do about building a tank for Bill. We won't turn this stuff out to range until you've dipped it."

CHAPTER
TWELVE

Flowering Love and Flying Lead

Three days after the new stock arrived at the Deep Springs ranch it was being dipped. The work was done in primitive fashion, it is true, for the tiny tank Lee had contrived was crude and hard to use, and only one cow at a time could be handled. When the work was completed, however, he pronounced it satisfactory.

It was late Sunday afternoon by that time. Any hope of seeing Kit, as he had planned, was gone now, but as he rode back to Grass Valley with Brett he announced his intention of going to the Painted Meadows the following morning.

"If it's all right with you, Uncle Jim, I'll get an early start and go into Powder City after I've stopped at the station. I haven't been in town since I got back. I'll come up tomorrow night. Mother must be home from the hot springs. I'd like to spend an hour or two with her."

"Take your time, you don't have to hurry," Brett told him. "Has it occurred to you that you may be forbidden to enter the house?"

"Why, no!" The suggestion startled Lee and he did not try to conceal the fact. "Dad couldn't go that far — deny me the right to see my mother."

160

"I sincerely hope that won't be the case," said Jim. "I'll have some letters for you to take in; we've got to do something about a new brand and have some irons made. I don't want anything unusual. Diamond B would suit me, but if I filed for it I'd most likely be told someone was using it and have to go through the whole thing a second time. How does J Bar B strike you?"

"Sounds fine," said Lee.

"That'll be it, then." Jim shook his head regretfully. "It'll take me some time to get used to it."

This was the second time since the middle of the week that Lee had made the long trip between the ranches. The prophylactic medicines he needed for the dipping-bath not being available at Deep Springs, he had been compelled to return to Grass Valley for them. On that occasion he had encountered several of Edwards's neighbors. They had some news of Stash, transmitted via the range grapevine. He had seen the Twin Buttes drive well on its way up the eastern slope of the Big Medicines, and he was last reported to be at the Kelly Creek ranch.

Lee also learned that Ben Lafoon had been laid to rest in the Powder City cemetery. No arrests had been made in connection with the murder. Marsh Effingham was still working on the case, but the Deep Springs cowmen expected little or nothing to come of it. As one said, "If anythin' is done, we'll have to do it."

Time was already working against them, Lee thought, dulling the edge of their vengeance. Their hatred of Stash was as implacable as ever, but there was a difference: they no longer had what they felt was the threat of the all-powerful Brett-Cameron Company to unite them.

It was not yet dark when Lee and Brett rode into the yard at Grass Valley. Half a dozen broncs stood tethered at the hitch rail, bedrolls draped across the saddle bows. Lee understood what it meant.

"Looks like Bill knew what he was talking about when he said you'd have all the men you needed," he observed with a smile.

"Seems so," Brett murmured, pleased at this evidence of loyalty to him. "They took a chance, throwing up their jobs before they knew whether I could use them. I guess they knew I wouldn't turn them away."

These recruits were from Kelly Creek and Twin Buttes, men who had worked long and faithfully for Jim. Late as the hour was, they still sat in the dining-room with the Grass Valley crew, the talk the merriest the house had heard in months.

"What seems to be the reason for this?" Jim inquired, pretending not to know why they were there.

"Boss, it means we're throwin' in with you, whether it means wages or just grub fer us," Curly Deshong answered. Brett had often called Curly the best bronc-buster in Wyoming. "There'll be a couple Ruby Lake boys showin' up yet tonight. In other words, we're workin' fer you or we ain't workin'."

"By Joseph, you'll think you've been working before roundup time rolls around!" Jim told them with a grin. "I appreciate this, boys. I can't use all of you here; I'll have to send some of you over to Deep Springs."

162

The men kept up a running fire of conversation with him as he and Lee ate supper. After the crew filed out Jim got pen and paper and wrote his letters.

Lee left immediately after breakfast. By high noon he was on the Painted Meadows. Only then did it occur to him that he might not find Kit at the station.

He was to be spared that disappointment. Almost as soon as he turned off the road she was at the door, waving to him.

"I was beginning to wonder if you'd forgotten me," she said reprovingly as he got down and took her hands.

When Lee attempted to apologize for his seeming neglect, she stopped him, "I didn't mean that, Lee. I heard through Vangie that you were at Deep Springs, busy as a beaver. I knew I'd be seeing you as soon as you could make it."

"If wishing could have brought me I'd have been here every day," said Lee. "So much has happened since I saw you last. I'd planned to get down yesterday, but it was so late when we got through there wasn't any chance."

Kit gave him a smile that was reward enough for the long miles he had come. "You're here, that's all that matters. Put up your horse and I'll ask you in. I haven't had lunch, and I'm sure you haven't."

Lee tethered his bronc and watered it. Kit stood with her back against the hitch rail, waiting for him to finish. Her smile had fled and her eyes were tender and grave as she watched him.

Lee turned unexpectedly and caught her in that position, her elbows on the rail, her breasts standing out firmly and her mannish shirt and tight-fitting Levis sharply outlining the perfection of her slim figure. With her head thrown back, her lips slightly parted, and her eyes wistful and moody, she had never seemed so desirable to him. The impulse to take her in his arms and crush his lips against hers almost overwhelmed him. A faint sigh escaped Kit. It sobered him.

"What is it?" he asked. "You were so gay and happy a moment ago."

"I'm frightened. I can't help it. Having you here safe and well only makes me ask how it will be the next time. Things have been happening so fast, and you always seem to be in the center of them. What will next week bring — and the next?"

He tried to convince her that everything would work out for the best. She was well informed, and the source of her information surprised him.

"Don't worry about it," he urged. "The break had to come. I knew you'd hear about what had taken place, but I never figured you'd get it direct from Father."

"I met him on the road that morning, Lee. He was on his way back to town from Grass Valley. I couldn't help noticing that something unusual was wrong. I asked about you, and that was too much for him; he told me everything. Parting company with Mr. Brett after all these years would have been bad enough, but what he can't get over is that you've let him down."

Lee's face thinned and he gazed at her in tight-lipped silence for a moment. "I haven't let him down, Kit. Far from it. I'm sorry if you think I dogged it. You wouldn't feel that way if I could give you my reasons."

"Does that mean it's something I shouldn't know, Lee?"

"It's something I don't want you to know. Are you disappointed in me?"

"I expected you to stand up to Stash and fight him. I don't necessarily mean with your fists or guns; there were other ways to knock the conceit out of him. It wouldn't have taken you long to convince him and everyone else that you'd be the one to take your father's place. He'll have everything his own reckless way now. Nothing will be too foolhardy for him to attempt."

"Kit — can't I make you understand that my hands were tied?" Lee demanded earnestly, stung by her criticism. "I didn't step out because I wanted to. If I'd had only myself to think about, I'd have given Stash a battle. I know I've hurt Father. But it could have been worse for him and a million times worse for Mother."

A chilling sort of understanding flashed through Kit. She had heard the ugly gossip that connected Stash with the killing of Ben Lafoon. Vangie Edwards and the Comerford twins had all but accused him of it. It was so unthinkable to her that she had refused to accept it as anything more than the prejudiced, irresponsible chattering of the girls, who consciously or otherwise were enlarging on what they heard at the family table. And yet, for all its guarded vagueness, she knew Lee was telling her that he was shielding Stash. Shielding him from what? She didn't have to ask herself that question; there was only one conclusion she could

165

draw. It was terrifying, and she trembled under its impact.

"Lee, I'm sorry — so sorry," she cried. "Forget everything I said. Forgive me if you can. I want you to have success, Lee, be all I know you can be. I couldn't bear the thought that you had thrown your chances away without putting up a fight for them."

"If we understand each other, that's all that's necessary," said he. He spoke with a sternness that was faintly reminiscent of his father. "We'll say no more about it. I hope there'll never be any need to bring it up again. I'm not starting from scratch with Jim Brett; he's taking me in as a junior partner. I'll share in the profits and turn part of my share back into the ranches and build up an interest in them. But I'm not giving up on my science and animal medicine. Just making money won't satisfy me; I want to do something for this country. In another two weeks we'll be into the hot weather. It won't be long after it gets here before Vangie's father and a good many independent cowmen will be beating a trail to Grass Valley to ask me to do something. They all buy southern cattle, even if it's only a handful, and every last one of them always has trouble with Texas fever. I'll do what I can. It won't be much — it'll be too late to stamp it out this year — but I'll prove even to Stash that I know what I'm talking about."

His face had lost its sober lines, and the boyish enthusiasm Kit so admired in him was bright in his eyes.

166

"You'll have success, and it won't spoil you, Lee. In one way or another you'll be a big man in this part of Wyoming some day. Will you please remember that I was the first to tell you so?"

Her mood had changed and she had recaptured her usual gaiety.

"There's a coffeepot boiling over somewhere, young lady!" Lee informed her.

"Definitely!" she agreed, sniffing the air. "Give me your arm, milord, and we'll see what can be done about it."

They hurried in and Kit ran to the kitchen.

"I don't see your father around," Lee called to her.

"He went down to Salt Lake City to lecture at the University. He'll be home tomorrow evening . . . Are you going on into town?"

"That was my intention," he answered from the kitchen doorway. "I thought I'd take a chance on finding Mother had been brought home. I'd like to see her."

"She came back yesterday, Lee. I was in Powder City in the morning, taking Father to the train. When I went up to the house Dr. Wilkins was there and he asked me not to disturb your mother. She was sleeping."

"What did Doc have to say?" Kit had foreseen the question and dreaded it. "Does he think she's any better?"

"He refused to be pinned down," she replied, wanting to spare him a more honest answer. "You know how doctors are."

167

Lee wasn't deceived. "Looks bad, I guess. Mother hasn't been well for years; it can't go on much longer . . . Don't bother about lunch; a sandwich and coffee will do me. If it's all right with you, I'll only stay a few minutes now and stop in this evening for an hour or two on my way home."

"Why, of course," Kit said. "You go into town now. I'll be looking for you about eight o'clock. I'm making a new dress. I'll finish it and be all prettied up for you."

She could never be any prettier than she was at the moment, Lee told himself.

When he arrived in Powder City the bank had closed for the day, but his father had not had time to reach home. Lee wanted him to be there, to either deny or grant him permission to enter the house. With time to kill, he spent half an hour in a barbershop. When he came out he decided to leave his horse at the rack and walk home.

Morgan and Doc Wilkins sat on the porch. They saw Lee coming and held a hasty conference. Morg got to his feet and disappeared into the house.

"Does this mean I'm not going to be allowed to see Mother?" Lee inquired.

"No, you can see her for a few minutes," Doc informed him. "But sit down, Lee. There's a couple things I want to say to you. The time has come for plain speaking. I kept the truth back from your father as long as I could. He knows what the situation is now, and I think you should know . . . Your mother is not going to get well, my boy. What she has always called her

168

lumbago long ago became a chronic rheumatic fever. It's begun to attack the heart valves. When she goes, she'll go quickly."

Though he was prepared for bad news, Lee winced unashamedly. "When, Doc?" he asked grimly.

"A week or two — a month. It won't be long. I think she knows, but you'd never guess it. Your mother is a gallant old soul, Lee. I have a nurse for her, and I drop in two or three times a day. Your father hasn't said a word to Mattie about breaking with Jim or about the trouble between you and Stash. So far as she knows everything's as it was. I don't want you to let the cat out of the bag; if we can't do anything else for your mother, we can at least give her some peace of mind. She's in her room. You go up. I'll give you a little time. When I walk in that'll be the signal for you to leave."

Lee found a marked change in his mother; she was thinner and her eyes were overbright. She tried to raise herself for his embrace but lacked the strength to do it. The nurse left the room, and they talked for a few minutes. Mattie refused to discuss what she called her "condition."

"I know everything possible is being done for me," she murmured. "Your father and the nurse wait on me hand and foot . . . It makes me happy to know you and Stash are getting along together, Lee. Your father tells me you have dipped some of the new cattle. It'll be wonderful if you've found a way to prevent tick fever. Years ago, when we were living at Grass Valley, it seemed that every day during July and August stock had to be destroyed."

This was a safe topic, and Lee talked freely.

"You don't know how proud we are of you," she told him. "Your father often speaks of what you are going to accomplish. I don't say anything to him, Lee, but he's worrying about something. There're lines in his face that I used not to see there. I wish you'd look after him a little bit and try to get him not to work so hard."

"I'll speak to him, Mother," he promised.

"And Kit — have you seen her recently?"

"Just a few hours ago. I'm going back to the ranch this evening. I'll stop in on my way up. She asked about you."

"She's a fine girl, Lee. She was here yesterday but the doctor wouldn't let her see me. I wish you'd ask her to come again. This spring when the weather was so bad she used to come, and it was just like the sunshine came in with her . . . She's very fond of you, my boy."

"I'm more than fond of her, Mother. I'm going to ask her to marry me as soon as I know how everything's going to work out."

"What do you mean — work out?" Mattie was quick to ask. "It can't be money —"

"I — I meant how things work out with the cattle. I want to prove I know what I'm talking about." He realized he had come close to tripping himself.

The moment stayed with him long after he had left town on his way north. They might keep his mother from knowing how matters stood between his father and Stash and himself, but surely they never could have kept her in the dark if Stash had been brought to trial for murder. That knowledge fortified Lee in the stand he had taken. "It was the only thing to do, and I'm glad I had the nerve to go through with it!"

He was aware of the two horsemen, who had drawn off the road in front of the station, some time before he came up to them. He stiffened in the saddle and felt a cold chill of alarm run down his spine when he recognized Duke Rucker and Bill Dent. A quick glance at the station revealed a horse standing at the rack. Lee didn't have to identify the animal to be sure his brother was here.

Duke and Dent threw their broncs across the lane, barring the way. They expected words from Lee. If Stash needed to be warned, an argument would do it. But believing Kit to be in danger snapped all restraint in Lee. Instead of words, they got his gun.

"Get 'em up," he rapped. "This thing shoots when you squeeze the trigger."

Rucker and Dent needed a moment to shake off their surprise. Slowly they raised their hands. Lee got their guns and tossed them off into the brush. His face was hard and flat, and so was his voice.

"I don't know what Stash is up to! If it's anything like what I think it is, he'll settle with me, and so will you lice. I'm going to start counting. If you're in sight when I reach ten, I'll bust you, so help me God!"

"That .45 looks like the high card around here," Duke growled. "Come on, Bill, we'll drift!"

They jogged down the road and Lee drove on to the station and flung himself from his horse. The door stood open. Stash's angry voice reached him.

"I won't take that for my answer!" Lee heard him insist. "I'm setting on top of the heap now, and it wasn't any accident. What do you think I been fighting for? I didn't want money just for myself — I wanted it for you! There's nothing to the dirty talk about me having Lafoon knocked off. Why should you believe it? Let a few weeks pass and you won't hear no more about it."

"I don't want to hear any more!" Kit cried. "I told you not to come here again! Take your hands off me, Stash!"

"No, I won't. I'm going to make you listen to me."

Something in Kit's eyes swung him around. Lee stood in the doorway, tall and wide, his face lean and rocky. Stash's lip curled away from his teeth in a wolfish snarl.

"So it was you she's all dolled up for!" Stash took one step to his right and his hand dropped like a plummet. "We'll settle this right now!"

The red fury of Lee's gun stopped him, the slug slapping into Stash's left shoulder and half turning him around. In the low-ceilinged room the shot roared like thunder. The night wind caught the trailing blue smoke and whisked it out of the window.

Kit didn't scream. Her face white beneath its tan and make-up, she stood there not moving until Lee spoke to her.

"Unbuckle his gun belt and let it drop on the floor. I ought to kill him. If he moves a finger, I shall!"

Stash kept his eyes on Lee, watching him like a hawk. A widening crimson circle began to stain his shirt. This was the second time in less than a week that he had stopped a bullet. He didn't know how his brother had got past Rucker and Dent, but he wondered about it and swore to himself they'd answer for it.

Lee kicked gun and belt aside.

"You've got a horse," he said. "Get on it and get away from here. If you ever try to molest Kit again, I'll come after you and hell won't be big enough to hide you. Start loping!"

Stash managed a sneer that a stage villain would have envied. "You're making a mistake letting me go. I'll get you for this, and that's for sure."

"If you come after me, come yourself," Lee fired back. "Don't send Sixto Guerra."

Stash was swaggering to the door. It stopped him in his tracks to have Guerra's name thrown at him.

"I know — you don't have to ask," Lee ground out. "And I'm not the only one who knows. For Mother's sake, I broke with Dad; it wasn't to spare you. She's dying. Do anything to shame her before she goes and you're a dead rat. Now git."

Stash's mouth had lost its scornful grin. He forgot all about the pain in his shoulder as he stared at Lee. This, he realized, was not the same gentle, self-effacing younger brother whom he had always held in utter contempt. Feeling a respect born of fear, he reached his horse and spurred away.

His going released Kit from her spell, and she flung herself into Lee's arms and buried her head on his shoulder.

"My dear! My dear!" she cried. "I'm so frightened."

"Don't be," Lee implored, drawing her close. "He won't bother you again. Stash knows where he stands with me."

"Darling, he knows too much!" Kit insisted. "I can surmise what this man Guerra is and what use Stash made of him. You shouldn't have told him, Lee. He'll kill you if he can."

"No, Kit, I didn't say too much; I threw a scare into Stash that'll make him toe the line. He knows he's on shaky ground — why, he's afraid to ride alone at night. You leave the worrying to me."

He tilted her head and gazed at her fondly.

"Lee!" she whispered, her arms stealing about his neck. "Kiss me, darling, and tell me you love me."

He drew her closer and his lips found hers. The seconds slipped away unnoticed as she yielded to his caresses.

"To say I love you isn't enough," he murmured. "Seems as though you were a part of me — a part that's always been missing. I couldn't go on living without you. I told Mother this afternoon I was going to ask you to marry me. I'm asking you now, Kit. I know this is not your country. Life isn't so easy out here. But I'll make it up to you some way. Will you be my wife, Kit?"

She smiled at him with misty eyes. "Lee, I knew you would ask me some day; and I knew what my answer would be. My place is with you, here or anywhere!"

Happy as they were, they could not erase the violent scene with Stash from their minds. Lee stayed on and on until it was almost midnight, and still six hours of

174

riding ahead of him. Loath as she was to have him leave, Kit finally insisted it was time for him to go.

"Breakfast will be over before you get home," she told him. "And I presume you have a busy day ahead of you."

Lee laughed. "I'm so deliriously happy I'm not even thinking about tomorrow. But I'll go; I know you've got to be in town in the morning to meet your father. I don't expect him to be too happy about our plans. It's going to leave him alone, Kit."

They decided that during the lull in September, when the summer's work was done and before preparations for the roundup began, they would be married.

"Dad will take it in stride, as he does everything else," she declared. "If we're going to live at Grass Valley, I'll come down once a week and catch up on my work for him; and we can visit back and forth. While I'm in town tomorrow I'll see your mother. I'll remember what you told me and be careful not to disillusion her."

They stepped out together. Lee had Stash's gun in his holster. He had given Kit his own, though she had been reluctant to take it. He referred to it as he was leaving.

"If I thought you were ever to have need of it, I wouldn't leave you here alone. But keep it handy; it's always a comfortable feeling to have a little insurance."

He bent down from the saddle and, getting an arm around her waist, lifted her up beside him and kissed

her good night. Then without looking back he hurried
off into the night.

CHAPTER
THIRTEEN

Death Comes Quietly

Brett had no difficulty in registering the new J Bar B brand. On being notified that his request had been granted, he inserted the required legal notice necessary to establish his ownership of it in the Powder City *Gazette*. All other persons were forbidden under penalty of law to use the brand on livestock within the limits of the State of Wyoming.

Several days later the *Gazette* printed a similar notice, announcing that the Cameron Cattle Company had registered and was now the sole owner of the Three C (3 C) brand.

Then began the long, busy days at Grass Valley. Tiny Duprez, who doubled as ranch blacksmith, had hammered out a number of the new irons. To speed the work, the roundup wagon was sent out with the crew and they worked from it instead of returning to the house at night. Over at Deep Springs, Bill Morrow was similarly engaged.

Lee took it for granted that the various Cameron ranches were equally busy with the rebranding. Ten days passed in which he neither heard nor saw anything of Stash. His brother was keeping his distance from Kit,

177

too. By riding most of the night, Lee got down to spend an hour with her on two occasions. He chose to believe it wasn't only the press of work that was responsible for Stash's avoidance of further trouble.

"If he's wise, he'll continue to watch his step," Lee told Jim one evening as they sat in the dining-room at Grass Valley. "I guess he's smart enough to realize people have short memories. When I came through Deep Springs this afternoon I stopped at the post office for a few minutes. I talked to Vangie Edwards and a couple other people. Ben Lafoon's name wasn't even mentioned. I see by the *Gazette* that Effingham has called off his investigation and given up on the case. Neph Gibson and the Tumble L crew are the only ones who aren't forgetting."

"Gibson will never forget; he isn't built that way," Brett observed. "A little hotheaded but a good man, Neph. The last time I was in town I saw Guerra strutting up the street." He shook his head regretfully. "Seeing him go unpunished is a hard pill for me to swallow. But there's one thing about murder: time doesn't outlaw it ... Don't misunderstand me," he added quickly, seeing Lee's head go up. "I'm not thinking of backing out of my bargain. But I'd like to see that miserable little rat strung up by his neck!"

"So would I. It burns me when I think about it." Lee turned away and they said no more.

Another week saw the rebranding finished. The days continued to grow longer. The sun swung even higher and the winds that blew out of the southwest were hot and withering. The dry air lapped up every trace of

178

moisture. During the middle of the day tiny Grass Creek almost ceased to flow, so great was the evaporation. To escape the stifling heat of the bunkhouse, the crew carried their iron beds outside and slept in the yard.

"It's a hot spell, all right," Reb observed one morning as he and Lee stood watching the dust devils whirling over the flat where the old corral had stood. "Reckon if we're goin' to have some sick stock on our hands we'll know it in a few days now."

"It'll be the test," Lee agreed. He had put a small bunch of home-bred cows through the dipping-trough and placed them on the south range with the imported stock. "I don't expect to sail through without losing some stuff. But no matter how bad things get, you won't see any cows on the south range coming down with the fever. Dipping some of our own yearlings and putting them down there was an experiment. I knew I was putting my neck out when I made it. I'm willing to stand or fall on how it turns out."

He saw Kit and his mother over the week-end. Mattie was steadily losing ground. The signs were so unmistakable that it was unnecessary for Doc Wilkins to confirm the fact.

Lee caught a glimpse of his father, heavy-footed and looking older than his years, crossing the living-room and locking himself up in what he called "the library." (Except for several subscription sets, given away as premiums by a national weekly magazine, it was a library without books.)

When he returned to the ranch, Lee found Brett and Reb waiting for him. The foreman had two cows, both natives, penned up in the lower corral.

"They're showin' all the symptoms of tick fever," said Reb. "Top and Tiny picked them up on Buckshot Crick and put a rope on 'em and brought 'em in."

Lee went down to the corral at once. The cows felt hot. Their heads drooped. They would drink but wouldn't eat. They stood with backs humped, dull-eyed and not even interested in swishing their tails at the flies. Lee pronounced it Texas fever. He turned back the hair. Wherever he looked he found young ticks and only young ticks. These babies were the assassins. He looked further, trying to find adult ticks, especially old, bloated females. They were not there. It established a set of indisputable facts in his mind.

"The ticks on these cows are a carry-over from last year," he told Brett and Reb. "It stands to reason that most of the tick eggs that are still unhatched when the cold weather comes are winter-killed. Otherwise, the hordes of ticks we'd have today would have killed off all livestock a long time ago. Some of the eggs survive and hatch out when the spring sun gets warm. It isn't long before they're crawling up some cow's leg. That was the case here. I'd take an oath that these animals were perfectly healthy up to three weeks ago."

"I'll take your word for all that," said Jim. "These cows are sick. What I want to know is — can we save them?"

"I can tell you what our chances will be after. I've examined their blood. I'll take some samples right

180

away. And whatever you do, Reb, don't put any healthy stock in this corral. We'll have more sick cows. Pen them up in here. I'll keep the ground sprayed. I'm afraid we'll find some stock so sick it can't be moved. In that case it'll be too late to do anything. We'll have to destroy it and bury the carcasses."

Under the microscope the blood smears failed to reveal any wrecked corpuscles as yet. He looked at half a dozen smears before he was satisfied that the punched-out holes he had feared to find were not there. It was in those holes that the living microbes inevitably appeared.

He and Reb personally dipped the two cows and dragged them back to the corral. He knew they'd lose weight rapidly and apparently go from bad to worse for ten days. If they were alive then, they'd get well.

The two animals in the quarantined corral were joined by others. At one time there were over thirty fever-ridden cows penned up there. Several had to be shot. Out on the range others were destroyed. But the percentage remained favorable; of the cattle that were stricken, five survived for every one that had to be killed.

"It's bad," Jim confided to Lee "but nothing to compare with what it's been other years. It's the same story at Deep Springs. Bill swears that dipping and segregating the new stock did the trick. I've got to agree with him, Lee. That stuff on our south range is as fat and sassy as can be."

"No ticks down there, Uncle Jim." The fight wasn't over, but Lee knew he had won it and he was too elated to make any attempt to conceal the knowledge.

"Next year we dip every head of stock on the two ranches," said Jim. "That's how much you've convinced me. What'll be the best time to do it?"

"In the spring, right after the calf gather. It wouldn't hurt to dip the stuff late this fall and again in May. We could face the hot weather then knowing we didn't have a square foot of dangerous range. Once the tanks are in, the expense is slight. You never trim down your crew after the roundup. Labor wouldn't be a problem."

Jim wanted a tank built at the Deep Springs ranch similar to the one they had at Grass Valley. If work was not begun on it until after the roundup, he doubted that it could be completed in time to carry out the program Lee had suggested.

"The snow flies early in this country. We don't want to get caught. I can have the material on hand 'most any time. But you're going to be away for a couple weeks next month, when things slack off, and I'd like to have you superintend the job."

"Bill Morrow can handle it as well as I," Lee argued. "About all I did was draw the plans. We'll be going to Deep Springs in a day or two. We can take the plans along and talk things over with Bill."

"All right," Brett agreed, after some deliberation. "Seems you always get your way with me and it always turns out to be the right way. Make out a list of the material we'll need."

182

News of the success the J Bar B ranches were having in combating the annual fever epidemic traveled far and wide. It brought Charlie Edwards and Pete Hoffman to Grass Valley one morning to seek Lee's advice and help. Their herds were being ravaged.

"It's worse this year than last," Pete declared. "It's hit all of us around the Springs. From what I hear, it's worse than bad up above at Twin Buttes and Ruby Lake. At least it's bad enough to bring your old man up there."

"Is that so?" Lee remarked, recalling the derision with which his brother had greeted everything he had to say on the subject. Evidently Stash wasn't laughing so loud now. "Do you know what they're doing about it, Pete?"

"Young Oatwine, the forest ranger, came down from the reserve day before yesterday. He told me they'd dammed up that little crick by the house and dumped in a barrel of sheep dip and were drivin' stock back and forth acrost it. But the dam was leakin' like hell and your old man was runnin' the crew ragged tryin' to git them to keep the holes plugged up. I ain't heard what they're doin' at Ruby Lake. Shootin' stock, I reckon, same as we been doin'. Ain't there some serum we can shoot into the cattle to keep this thing from spreadin'?"

Lee shook his head. "You could pump them full of dope and it wouldn't do a bit of good. As Jim and everyone on this ranch has heard me say so often, the fever microbe is in the blood, breaking down the cells and turning the blood to water. You've got to kill the ticks before they have time to shoot those bugs into a cow. Dipping is the only way it can be done."

"But you can wait so long that even dipping is useless," Brett asserted. "I've had that proved to me."

"You make it sound hopeless, Jim," Edwards declared soberly. "We came over thinkin' Lee might be able to suggest somethin'. It's terrible to have to stand by like this, doin' nothin'."

"You're bound to lose more stock," said Lee. "On the other hand, it's never too late to dip healthy cattle. We've got a makeshift tank at the Deep Springs ranch that we won't be using again; we're going to put in a permanent one this fall. I'm sure Jim will let you have the one that's there now. It'll serve the purpose. It can be knocked down quickly and put up some place where all of you can use it."

Brett agreed readily to this, and Lee said he'd be on hand to mix the dip.

"Don't lose an hour if you can save it," he told them. "And when you've got the tank set up, keep it in operation day and night until you're finished. I know you all have some winter range. No matter how it pinches you later on, you've got to use it now. Dip a bunch of cows and put them on it at once; don't wait till you've run all your stock through the tank."

Edwards and Hoffman didn't relish the thought of using their winter range in early August. But this was an emergency, and Lee had given them a ray of hope. They voiced their appreciation and thanked Brett for his generosity.

184

Before the week was out the transplanted tank was going full blast, twenty-four hours a day. It wasn't long thereafter before the herculean task began to pay dividends. A break in the weather helped matters.

Lee arose one morning to find that the wind had swung around to the north. It was a good sign, and at breakfast he didn't hesitate to prophesy that the peak of the epidemic had passed.

Reports reaching Grass Valley soon bore this out. The Cameron ranches had been hit hardest of all. Lee didn't gloat over the fact; it was no satisfaction to him to know his father had lost so heavily. As far as Stash was concerned, however, Lee felt completely vindicated.

The irony of the situation bit deeply into Morgan Cameron. His son had come home equipped with knowledge acquired at his expense, and every stockman on the range had benefited by it but himself.

Customers at the bank found Morg a dour, brooding man, shorter of speech and temper than ever. Only to Old Stony did he unburden his mind. The ever faithful Stony often sat with him in his office after the bank closed, adversity only bringing them closer together.

Stony came in one afternoon with some news. Sixto Guerra had just left town to join the crew at 3 C's Ruby Lake ranch. Morg blew up immediately.

"What's Stash thinking of, taking on that little blackleg?"

"It's no more'n he's been doin' for weeks," Stony replied. He was incensed too. "He's let good men go and replaced 'em with range scum that Jim Brett wouldn't waste spit on. Yuh tell me he ain't to be trusted, yet yuh string along with him. I don't know why."

"Because I'm stuck with him!" Morg had been at some pains to learn the meaning of the gunshot wound in Stash's shoulder, and while Kit had been reluctant to speak frankly his imagination had filled in the gaps between her story and what he got out of Stash. "Lee should have killed him instead of just winging him! I wouldn't give the tip of Lee's finger for the whole of that pigheaded ass!"

"If yuh won't turn him adrift and git shet of him, what yuh goin' to do?"

"I'm going to clip his wings. I'll take time away from the bank and see for myself how things are being run out on the range."

Stony shook his head. "Yuh can't do that, Morg. Mattie'd smell a rat in a minute if yuh was away from town for two-three days at a time. Before yuh was through, yuh'd have to tell her ever'thin'."

It was true, and Morg didn't even attempt to deny it. But he refused to consider himself completely impotent. With a flash of his old authority, he ordered Stony to start for Ruby Lake at once.

"If Stash ain't there, you keep on going till you catch up with him. Tell him I want him here as quick as he can come. No excuses, Stony; he's to drop whatever he's doing and head for town. I'll put him on a short rein or know why."

Stony left the bank, grumbling to himself. For almost the first time in his life he found his convictions

186

running counter to Morgan Cameron's expressed words. *Bringin' Stash in fer another dressin' down won't do no good. He ain't hirin' men like Guerra to work cattle. He's got somethin' else up his sleeve that'll make more trouble for his father.*

The faithful Stony spat out an oath. "By grab, it's too damned bad he wa'n't drownded the day he was born!"

A thought he had contemplated before lodged in his mind. It was nothing less than that he take it upon himself to stop Stash. He scowled over it, his eyes dark and obscure in his grizzled face. He knew there was a limit beyond which he'd permit no one to hurt Morg Cameron. Stash was edging close to that invisible line. It might become necessary to kill him.

Stony considered it at length and without a trace of compunction. *That would be one way to handle it — mebbe the best way,* he decided. *He won't have to step over the line — jest tech it!*

He had to go all the way to Iron Point to find Stash. He was back in town with him two mornings later, only to learn that still another calamity had befallen Morgan Cameron and that the purpose for which Stash had been brought in had given way to one of quite another nature.

News of what had happened reached Grass Valley in the middle of the afternoon. Lee was in the yard, about to mount and ride to Buckshot Creek to inspect some cows, when he saw a horseman moving up the road at a swinging gallop. Arrested by the haste of this unknown rider, he waited for him to pull in. To his amazement he

187

saw it was Kit. He ran to her as she reined up, anxiety whipping through him.

"Stash?" he questioned tensely, his first thought being that his brother had visited the station again and molested her in some way.

Kit shook her head sadly. "No, Lee, it's your mother. She died just after midnight."

Though it was no less than he had expected would happen, it shook him to learn that his mother was actually gone.

Kit got down and put her arms around him. "I know you loved her, Lee. So did I. She just went to sleep; that was all. Your father wanted you to know."

"And he had to ask you to make this long ride? It's tough enough for a man."

"I didn't come alone. Stony's down the road at your line. Your father sent him, but he warned him that he wasn't to set foot on this ranch. When Stony stopped at the station to give me the news and I heard what his instructions were, I saddled my horse and came along. The funeral will be held tomorrow afternoon at two. When will you be in, Lee?"

"I'll go back with you and Stony. You'll want to rest an hour."

"No, I'm not tired. I thought I'd get back to town as soon as I could and go up to the house. Someone has to take charge of things there. People will be coming in every few minutes. Your father won't be able to look after everything."

"Where's Stash?"

"He got in this morning. He'll be no help at all."

188

"He isn't likely to be," said Lee. "Give me a few minutes to change. I'll leave word for Jim; he'll want to attend the funeral . . . I'd ask you to come in, Kit, but there isn't a comfortable chair in the house. You're sure you won't have some coffee and a bite to eat?"

"No, just some water. I'll get it at the pump." She gave him a tender, affectionate smile. "I know this is a blow to you. Don't take it too hard, dear. I'll always remember how happy your mother was when I told her we were to be married."

Lee steadied himself. "I'm glad she knew. I realize this is something I've got to get used to. I'll be all right when I've had time to pull myself together. You make yourself at home, Kit. I'll be just a few minutes."

Though it was nearing midnight when they reached town, a number of people were still at the house. It was the custom in Powder City to sit up with the dead. In the rear, at the entrance to the barn, someone was pacing back and forth, his cigarette glowing in the darkness. Lee looked closer and saw it was Stash.

Turning the horses over to Stony, Lee and Kit entered the house by the side porch. Doc Wilkins met them at the door and they spoke for a minute. Kit told him she was there to stay until the funeral was over.

"We certainly need someone to help out," said Doc. "I had Miss Hoskins stay on. Your Aunt Min and Aunt Rose arrived from Rawlins late this afternoon, Lee. They're both elderly, you know, and they went to pieces. I was glad I had a nurse here. She's had her hands full all day."

"What about Father?" Lee asked.

"I took him upstairs a couple hours ago and ordered him to bed. He's dropped off to sleep. The house is filled up, Kit. I'm afraid you'll have to share a room with Miss Hoskins." He glanced at Lee. "I suppose you'll want to go to the hotel."

"Naturally," was the clipped answer. "I want you to go out to the kitchen, Kit, and fix yourself something to eat before you do anything else. I'll see you before I leave."

The hour that followed was an unhappy one for him, made doubly so by the tears and lamentations of his mother's sisters, who were almost strangers to him, and the expressions of sympathy from the others present. He knew this talk was well meant, but he would have preferred to sit there alone with Mattie. Kit was finally able to rescue him.

"I know you want to be by yourself," she said. "And you need some rest. I'll look after your father, Lee. If he should ask to see you, what shall I tell him?"

"No," he replied, his mouth hard, "that won't happen. If you knew him as well as I do you wouldn't even suggest it as a possibility. Father won't unbend. He'll draw back into his shell further than ever now."

Whether the passing of Mattie Cameron would or would not heal the breach between Morg and Lee was a topic of wide speculation in Powder City. Some held that it would, but the majority took the opposite view.

When the services at the church were concluded and the mourners formed a procession to follow the casket to the cemetery, any doubt of the outcome quickly vanished. Stash walked with his father. Behind them came Mattie's sisters and other, more distant relatives. Far back, and definitely ignored, came Lee, with Kit at his side. Half a hundred others fell into line haphazardly. Few noticed that Jim Brett and Old Stony had paired off.

It was not without some embarrassment that Jim and Stony found themselves together. Scarcely a word passed between them until they were at the grave.

"Mattie was a good woman," Stony observed, his grim visage rockier than ever.

"She was," Jim agreed. "Morgan will miss her. I hate to see him left alone like this."

There was no rancor in his tone. Stony was surprised no little.

"Yuh bear him no grudge, Jim?"

"No," Brett replied. "The settlement the lawyers reached was satisfactory to me."

"I wa'n't speakin' of money. Behind his back things has been done in his name that's turned a lot of folks ag'in him. I figgered yuh was one of 'em."

"That's not the case, Stony. A certain party used to have me in the same fix he's got Morgan in. You know where to lay the blame, and so do I."

Stony nodded grimly. His narrowed eyes searched across the crowd and fastened on Stash. "The rotten, wuthless skunk! One of these days someone oughta step out and finish him off."

"Someone will," Jim said quietly.

The old man swung around and eyed him suspiciously, afraid lest he had given himself away. "What makes yuh so sure?"

"A lot of things changed when Mattie died . . . A lot of things, Stony!"

CHAPTER
FOURTEEN

Morg Cameron's Game

Back at Grass Valley, Brett said nothing to Lee about coming forward with the evidence they had against Guerra and Stash. It would be better, he decided, to give Lee a chance to bring it up himself, or at least to wait until time had dulled the shock of losing his mother.

Another matter came up at once to engage their attention. It concerned the Tumble L, and it brought Edwards and Hoffman to Grass Valley again. This time they had Comerford with them. Lafoon's will had been probated. His sister was the sole heir, and she was offering the ranch for sale, either stocked or without cattle.

"The three of us would like to buy it," said Edwards, "but we haven't enough cash to swing the deal. We won't ask Morg Cameron for a loan. We know what his answer would be if we did. Would you be interested in buying a slice of the ranch? That's good range below Buckshot Crick. You're familiar with it."

"I might be interested." Jim was hard put to conceal his eagerness. Years before he had made Lafoon an offer for the range he had foreseen the necessity of acquiring

193

it if Grass Valley was to realize its full worth. The quarrel that had ensued, ending in the death of Lafoon, had left him believing his chance of getting it was gone forever. He had known Tumble L would be sold some day and had taken it for granted that it would go as a whole.

"The price is right," Comerford stated. "We've got the figgers here and a map of how we aim to split things up. If you'll take the three thousand acres below Buckshot, we'll whack up the rest between us."

"What about the cattle?" Lee inquired. "You buying the bare ranch?"

"That's somethin' else to consider," said Pete. "Neph brought the stuff through in purty good shape. Lost about seventy head, he says. What's left is good Hereford stock. Ben was always buyin' good breeding-cattle. Between the three of us we can dig up money enough to take fifteen hundred head, if the price is what we figger it should be. We ain't talked that over with Mrs. Henley. If we took fifteen hundred, it'd leave about as many more for you to take over. Is that too many for you?"

"No, not if I buy more range. Let me look at these figures a minute and see how the lines would run if we cut up the ranch."

He retired to Lee's room, and the latter got what additional information he could from the Deep Springs men. Without warning, the conversation took a surprising turn.

"You saved the day for us, Lee," little Pete Hoffman declared, "and we ain't fergittin' it. We ain't fergittin' yore brother neither. He's been gatherin' a crew at Ruby Lake that's all gunslingers and the worst riffraff you ever laid eyes on. We figger he's lookin' ahead to the fall drive and intends to come bustin' through us with his beef."

"I don't know what else it could mean," Edwards added. "If that's his plan, he'll find us ready for him."

Lee had no solution to offer. "I don't pretend to know what Stash has on his mind. But if this deal goes through, we'll have some range east of Dutchman's Greek that he'd have to cross."

"I'd thought of that," Edwards told him. "Where will you and Jim stand on a proposition like that?"

Brett was in time to catch the question, and the matter had to be gone over a second time.

"I can give you our answer," Jim announced promptly. "Nobody's driving through our fence without permission. We'll fight him shoulder to shoulder with you . . . To get back to these papers. Everything looks all right to me. Is this Mrs. Henley at the Tumble L house now?"

Pete said yes. "She's anxious to get back to Cheyenne."

"Then I suggest that we ride over and have a talk with her. On account of the fever epidemic, stock is short in this country. She may feel she can get more if she sells her cattle at auction. We'll have to convince her she'll do better to come to terms with us. We can close the deal this morning if she's agreeable. We'll have a look at the stock before any money is passed to bind the sale."

They were able to make a satisfactory arrangement with Ben's sister, and after the terms had been agreed on Lee and Brett and the Deep Springs men were piloted over the Tumble L by Neph Gibson. They were pleased with what they saw. There was nothing left to do but return to the house and bind the deal with some cash and arrange to meet Mrs. Henley in Powder City the next day to have a lawyer draw up the necessary papers and file the deeds.

Neph didn't like the way things had gone and he made no bones about it. "I figgered when the place was sold I'd go with it," he said to Brett and Lee. "I can start lookin' for a job now."

"You've got a job with me, and at top wages, if you'll take it," Jim replied. "I've had my eye on you for years, Neph."

Gibson's forlorn look vanished in a twinkling. "I'm doggoned if it ain't nice of you to say that, Jim," he declared. "If you mean it, I'm your man."

"I always try to mean what I say," said Brett. "You keep your crew on till the first of the month. There'll be considerable work to be done. You can straw boss the job. After we get the stock parceled out it'll have to be rebranded. I'll have Reb send you over some men to give you a lift with that. In the meantime, I'll send a wagon and a fencing gang out to string wire between our new southeast corner and Edwards's line."

"That'll close the road about a mile and a half east of the Dutchman's Creek crossing!" Lee exclaimed, frankly surprised. "Is that your intention. Uncle Jim?"

196

"It will close it legally. We'll have between nine hundred and a thousand acres of fairly good graze below the road. It will be worthless to us if it isn't fenced in. We can't have stock drifting all over kingdom come. You may not know it, but when the county laid out that road it bought and condemned a right of way only as far as Dutchman's Creek; the roundabout road through Greely's Knob was supposed to serve the Deep Springs area. We'll put in a gate, same as Edwards did, and allow the road to be used; but it will be with our permission. I talked it over with Hoffman and Comerford and him. They agreed it was the thing for us to do."

Though the sale of the Tumble L ranch caused no excitement in Powder City, it did not go unnoticed by Morgan Cameron. He knew its new range and water rights would come close to doubling the earnings of Grass Valley. It irked him for a number of reasons, but principally because it had not come to pass in the days of Brett-Cameron. If it had, there would have been a different story to tell today.

Before the fence that was to close the Dutchman's Creek road was completed, Morg heard about it. It stirred him to action. Lee's activity on behalf of the Deep Springs stockmen during the fever epidemic, and the manner in which the Tumble L sale had been handled, were proof enough that the Brett forces and the cowmen for whom Edwards and Hoffman spoke had closed ranks and were prepared to stand together. Here was further proof of it.

Morg took the closing of the road as aimed primarily at him. It meant further strife, very likely bloodshed. He told himself he had had enough of fighting and incessant controversy. He brooded over it all evening as he sat in his office. Of late he had been spending his evenings at the bank, feeling less lonely there than at home.

A way to avoid hostilities and open the road occurred to him. He didn't question his ability to force it through.

"I'll be misunderstood and abused worse than ever for it," he mused. "But it will be for the good of everybody, and they'll realize it some day. I'll send word to the Dog Iron in the morning and tell Hutton to call a special meeting of the county commissioners."

That meeting was held behind locked doors, and it was a noisy, turbulent session. At its conclusion an announcement was forthcoming that caused consternation when it reached Deep Springs. Brett and Lee were summoned from Grass Valley. When they arrived at Edwards's house they found a score of cowmen gathered there.

"Jim, you've heard the news by now," Edwards said without preamble. "What are we goin' to do to stop it?"

"I don't know," Brett answered honestly. "I've thought about it all morning. If the county wants to build a road, from the creek to the Buttes, it's got the authority to do it. If we refuse to sell the land, it'll be condemned. By one means or another, they'll get a right of way."

198

"We been sold out," Pete raged. "This is Morg Cameron's work! He's got Hutton and the majority of the commissioners in the hollow of his hand. We was a pack of damned fools, figgerin' it was just Stash we was fightin'. This proves he's got the old man behind him."

"That's the way I see it," Dan Comerford spoke up. "If this wasn't Morg's idea, then he was talked into it by Stash."

"I'm afraid that's true," Brett was compelled to acknowledge. "The commissioners didn't take this action on their own hook. Beginning work at once gives the whole business an ugly look."

"I don't care how soon they start or how many men they put on the job, they won't build that road between now and the time snow flies," Comerford asserted.

"Course they won't — and they don't intend to!" Pete burst out with the vehemence that always characterized anything he said in excitement. "They'll survey it and git the stakes in. That'll do the trick. The road will be laid out, and when Twin Buttes and Ruby Lake and Kelly Crick get their beef cut ready, you'll see 'em drivin' right down through us. And 'cordin' to law they'll have the right to do it."

"Pull up the stakes as fast as they put 'em in the ground!" someone shouted from the back of the room. "That'll spike Morg Cameron's rotten game!"

To hear his father accused of such skulduggery and political corruption made Lee's blood run cold. And yet the evidence against him was such that he could not honestly tell these men they were mistaken. On the

199

other hand, he couldn't sit there and say nothing. He got to his feet and faced them.

"You just heard Jeff Henry say the way to beat this proposition is to pull up the stakes. We could get away with that for a day or two, then the sheriff would move in with a bunch of deputies and we'd be stopped cold. I don't know what we can do, but that certainly isn't the way to begin. I realize as well as you do that this decision to build a road due east from the crossing to Twin Buttes has my father's backing. I'm not trying to make excuses for him or suggesting that the commissioners were justified in taking this action, but the explanation they give has some truth in it. Maybe it's only the sugar coating to make the pill taste better. It's a fact, though, that for years the Deep Springs district has been crying that the county was neglecting it. It's an old story that the road around by Greely's Knob takes half a day longer to reach town than it should, that snow closes it for weeks at a time every winter. Those things are going to be raked up and used to turn sentiment throughout the county against us. If that succeeds, we won't be able to block the building of this new road for long, no matter what we do."

Pete was on his feet instantly. "We ain't ag'in' the idea of a new road. It's where they're puttin' it that we won't stand for. Why didn't they listen to what we had to say about it, 'stead of jammin' it down our throats this way?"

He glared about him fiercely, ready to answer his own question if no one else could.

"I can tell you why," said Jim. "They know we'd have told them to abandon the old road back to where it begins to swing north, and to strike east from that point. They'd have hit Dutchman's Creek about two miles above the present crossing. That would have given them nothing but wasteland ahead of them till they struck you. They wouldn't have needed a foot of our range and only the thinnest sliver of yours. You and Charlie have a fence between your places; the road could have followed the fence and hugged your lines until it hit Dan's ranch. A little job there would have run it past him without too much damage. If they laid it out along those lines, we'd have no kick coming. It wouldn't be as convenient for the Cameron ranches as for us, but they could make good use of it."

"Then in God's name tell me why the commissioners voted to cut across your range and split my ranch in two!" Edwards burst out. "It'll hit Pete hard too, and Comerford. The road will have to be fenced off. The county won't foot the bill for it, either. They'll pay forty per cent and we'll be stuck for the balance!"

"Economy will be the excuse, Charlie. I reckon we're pretty well agreed on what the real reason is. However that may be, if you feel about it as I do, we'll fight this thing to a finish."

A rousing chorus of approval greeted Brett.

"But Lee is right," he continued, "pulling up the stakes or trying to run off the surveyors won't get us anywhere. We'll have to do our fighting inside the law."

"You ain't suggestin' that we appeal to the commissioners or try to get an injunction, be you?"

Dan Comerford questioned, his sarcastic tone saying plainly enough what he thought about proceeding in that fashion.

"Indeed I'm not," Brett informed him. "Appealing to the commissioners would be a waste of breath. If we asked Abernathy for an injunction, we'd never get it. Morgan Cameron is too strong in that quarter. The thing for us to do is make it impossible for the road to be laid out until the fall elections. That'll give us a chance to vote into office a couple men from this end of the county who will see things our way."

"How we goin' to hold it off?" Pete growled. "What's your scheme?"

"Well, a man can be arrested and fined for obstructing a county project, but I never heard of a cow being hailed into court for such an offense." Jim smiled grimly. "There's no law on the books that can tell me where I have to graze my stock. If I want to move a thousand head down where this road is going through, that's my business. They'll be there, I can tell you, and I'll see that they're kept on the prod until they're good and spooky. If a couple surveyors can work through a herd of range cows that have been running wild all summer, they'll be free to try."

Pete and the others got the idea instantly.

"Dang my hide if that won't do it!" Comerford roared. "You'll run 'em ragged, Jim!"

"Don't leave it all up to me," Brett warned them. "They may try to jump ahead when they see we've got them stopped. We won't prevent them from crossing our range. Don't you stop them; but be ready for them

202

if they move up to your line. Throw so many cows in their way that they can't do a thing."

"By gravy, I've got a big red bull I'll sick on 'em," Pete chortled. "Those gents will light out for the nearest fence when that critter begins bellerin'."

They talked it over at length, Brett repeatedly stated that there must not be any violence.

"Pretend to be helpful, and don't get into any arguments with these men," he said again. "They'll undoubtedly call in the sheriff. Marsh will see through our game, but if we stay within our rights there isn't a blessed thing he can do!"

CHAPTER
FIFTEEN

Gunsmoke on the Graze

Before returning to Grass Valley, Brett and Lee spent some time watching the work on the new fence. The gate was in place already. A lot of wire remained to be strung. Jim ordered the pace stepped up.

"I want this job completed before you knock off tomorrow evening," he told Tiny, who was in charge of the fencing gang.

This was Friday. On Sunday morning Reb began moving cattle from the J Bar B south range to the trouble spot. Before nightfall he had upward of five hundred head on the new range. The rebranding was already in progress at the Tumble L, and Neph Gibson was ordered to have the cows driven into the road pocket as soon as they could be handled. Four men were to be stationed there, night and day.

"I'm going to send you down there," Jim informed Lee. "It's a ticklish job. I know I can depend on you not to lose your head. Take Tiny, Top, and Ryan with you. And you better take a cook outfit along and grub enough to last you some time. I'll be down every day and keep you supplied."

On Monday morning two surveyors and their rodmen arrived at the crossing and, after making camp, set up their transits and began running a line. Noon of the following day brought them to the new gate. Brett was there. The leader of the party, a man named Curtis, introduced himself.

"I'm sorry, Mr. Brett, but you'll have to get your cattle out of the way. We want to work across your range this afternoon."

"Well, that's an unusual request," Jim replied with well-feigned surprise. "These cows are not trespassing; they're on their own range."

"I'm aware of all that," said Curtis. "I'm not contending that you didn't have the right to close this old road."

"We haven't closed it, Mr. Curtis. The gate isn't locked. You have our permission to come through any time. But we don't propose to move our stock. We've just bought this range,, and we intend to use it."

They argued the matter for some minutes. The head of the surveying party began to lose his patience.

"I can't understand your headstrong attitude, Mr. Brett. I'm only asking you to move this stuff out of the way for a few hours. As soon as we get through you can graze your cows here to your heart's content."

Brett still said no.

"I can compel you to move them," Curtis threatened.

"On what authority?"

"On the authority of this county! The commissioners ordered this new road surveyed. You're making it impossible for us to proceed."

"If the county commissioners think they can compel us to work our cattle according to their whim, they're free to try," Brett answered. "I'm not from Missouri, but I'll have to be shown."

When he arrived on the scene the next morning he found the sheriff there.

After some preliminary skirmishing, Effingham said, "You're climbin' a slippery tree, Jim. I know what's behind this. You can't get away with it. The chairman of the board told me I was to try to get you to listen to reason, and if that didn't work I'd be sent back with a warrant."

Brett smiled. "That sounds more like Morg Cameron than Ab Hutton. But you go ahead and get your warrant, Marsh. You better get a flock of them while you're about it, and swear in a bunch of deputies to serve them on these cows. Some of them don't know how to read. You may have a time convincing the critters the law is talking to them . . . But seriously, Marsh, no one's going to put a hand on this stock without my permission. You know that. And after all these years you ought to know I don't scare worth a cent."

Effingham knew only too well. "It puts me in a hell of a hole," he growled. "Give you some cards and you always play a smart game."

He suggested a compromise.

"What sort of a compromise?" Jim inquired.

"Curtis says you agreed to let him through. Is that correct?"

"It is."

"Then I'm going to advise him to put his stuff in his wagon and drive around your herd and go to work on Edwards's range. He won't get nowhere stallin' around here, and I'll tell him so."

"That might be helpful," Jim declared with a straight face. "They say there's more'n one way to skin a cat."

Curtis accepted the sheriff's suggestion. He ordered camp struck. He piled his assistants into the wagon, and with Effingham piloting them they came through the gate and described a wide circle around the cattle.

"They'll be back before long," Lee predicted as he and Brett watched the wagon bouncing over the uneven range. "I rode over to Edwards's line last evening. He's got half of his herd pressed up against the fence and enough men on the job to hold them there."

Jim nodded. "We'll be seeing them about the middle of the afternoon. Marsh is going to be all het up over this."

Shortly after three o'clock they saw the wagon returning. The sheriff came on ahead, snorting with anger.

"Why'd you send me off on this wild-goose chase?" he demanded of Brett. "Why didn't you tell me you had the whole thing rigged? You knew Charlie was standin' by, ready to give us the same treatment you handed out. I suppose Pete Hoffman is waitin' at his line with more of the same."

"Don't take it too hard, Marsh," Brett advised calmly. "I wanted you to see for yourself that we don't take kindly to the idea of having our range cut up."

Marsh wasn't to be mollified.

"We'll see if you fellas can defy the whole county government! If Glen Richards can't dig into the law books and come up with somethin' that'll set you down on the seat of your pants, he oughta be run out of office." (Richards was the district attorney.)

Curtis and his party retired to the creek and set up camp again, there to remain until the commissioners cleared the way for them.

Three days passed without bringing any further action. Brett saw Pete and Edwards. All three agreed that the county commissioners had been stalemated.

"If there was anything they could do, we'd have felt it by now, with the *Gazette* playing the story up the way it has," said Jim. "I reckon they figure we'll get tired of tying ourselves up this way and all they've got to do is wait us out. Curtis is still camped at the crossing."

"They won't catch us nappin'," Edwards declared flatly. "I've got a lot of work to do, but this comes first!"

"You bet it does!" Pete agreed. "We're standin' pat, no matter how long it takes."

Night was falling when Brett got back to Grass Valley. He ate a late supper and was still at the table when Bill Morrow roared into the yard on a lathered horse. The way in which he burst into the dining-room told Jim at a glance that something was wrong.

"Jim, who have you got up at the old road?" Bill jerked out excitedly.

"Why, Lee's up there. He's got Top and Tiny and Ryan with him."

"Well, they're in trouble! I'm surprised you haven't heard the shootin'; the wind is this way. I figgered this was what was comin' up the second Curly brought word in this afternoon that he'd spotted Stash Cameron and the gang he's been gatherin' at Ruby Lake slippin' down through the Slate Hills! Curly counted a dozen of 'em, and he says there was more than that!"

Brett had leaped to his feet. With Morrow trailing behind, he ran outside. He had no trouble identifying the faint puffs of sound from the south as gunfire.

"I didn't lose no time gettin' here," Bill explained, catching his breath. "I saw Pete and told him what I figgered was up. He said he'd get word to Edwards."

Brett rushed to the bell rope. Grabbing it, he set the big ranch bell to clanging. It brought Reb on the run, and behind him the crew began spilling out of the bunkhouse.

"Saddle up! Have the men take their rifles!" Jim snapped the order at Reb. "Stash Cameron has jumped us down on the road. Get a man started for Tumble L. Whoever we've got there is to head for the road at once. Tell Neph I want him to take a hand. There must be some others over there who'll be glad to throw in with us. The more the better. Get moving! I'll be ready to ride with you!"

Reb whirled on his heels and ran down the yard, barking orders at the crew.

"Throw a saddle on a horse for me and get a fresh mount for yourself," Jim rapped out at Bill. "I'll get rifles for the two of us. This whole thing is my fault. All

209

my fault. I should have known Stash would pull something like this when he saw we had things tied up!"

A few minutes later every man on the ranch, save the cook and old Oddie, flashed out of the yard. At a driving gallop they thundered across the south range. The night was at its darkest, as was always the case on these high plains just before moonrise. Brett glanced hopefully to the east, but the horizon was still an unbroken line of blackness. The night didn't trouble the sure-footed broncs. With manes and tails flying they swept on, miraculously avoiding the gopher holes and patches of catclaw.

Gradually the stars came out, enabling a man to see a few feet. Every minute counted, and Brett heaved a sigh of relief when he and his men put behind them the old fence which for so many years had formed the southern boundary of the Grass Valley ranch. The sound of intermittent gunfire was distinctly audible now above the rumbling of shod hoofs. All were aware of it. They took what encouragement they could from the fact that someone was still able to carry on the fight. Presently, however, they met stampeding cattle. These were the cows that had been used to block the road. The frenzied animals passed them.

This left little to be surmised. Obviously Stash's gang had cut the fence, got behind the herd, and set it in motion. That Lee and his three men had found some sort of cover and were making a fight of it seemed equally plain.

210

A quarter of a mile above the road Brett called a halt. "Watch the gun flashes," he cried. "They'll give us an idea of what we're busting into."

"Someone's shootin' from near the gate!" Reb exclaimed. "There! Two flashes at the same time! That must be Lee and our boys!"

It was growing lighter all the time. To the east the moon was just beginning to peek over the horizon. From that direction came a sharp spluttering of shots.

"That'll be Pete and his crowd," said Morrow. "He's had time to get organized and be movin' up. Figure out how we're goin' to play this, Jim, and I'll go over and tell Pete what you want him to do."

"Time enough for that when we've got Lee's bunch out of this," Brett replied. "Is that them down at the gate, Reb?"

"It sure is. They overturned the wagon they brought down and they're firin' from behind it. They're cornered there. If they try to drop back, they'll be picked off."

The revealing gun flashes had by now established the position of the attackers. Sweeping across the road and charging into them promised to be so costly that Jim wouldn't consider it. But to rescue the besieged men at the wagon box called for a diversionary move of some sort.

"A bluff might do the trick," Morrow suggested. "If we tear in with guns blazin', like we mean business, that gang may give ground. Whether they do or not, we can at least keep 'em busy till we pick up the boys. Soon as we have, we can fall back."

211

Jim thought it over for a moment. He had no better idea to advance.

"All right," he declared soberly. "We'll try it. You know without my telling you that this gang of gunmen will shoot you down if they get the chance. Remember that, and when you shoot, shoot to kill. Now spread out some and get your guns ready. When I raise my hand, we'll go."

"Jim, it ain't necessary for you to mix in this," Morrow protested. "You hang back; we'll handle it."

"No," Brett said firmly. "I've never asked a man to do what I wouldn't do myself . . . Get ready!"

CHAPTER
SIXTEEN

An End to Violence

Guns cracking, their ponies guided only by the pressure of their knees, they charged hell-bent for the road. Stash and his hired warriors shifted their fire from the wagon box to meet this new threat. Their first shots were high, then they began to get the range. A horse went down. The rider leaped clear and began firing from the ground.

Slugs clipped Dex Ferris and another man before the charge reached the road. The damage was slight, and they plunged on with the others. The pattern of fire from the enemy changed abruptly, indicating that J Bar B's guns were speaking with some authority or that Stash was realigning his men.

This break, brief as it was, gave the Grass Valley crew the advantage, and they made the most of it. They swept up to the gate. Willing hands plucked Lee, Tiny, and Ryan out from behind the wagon box and carried them back to safety while some of the other Grass Valley men covered the withdrawal.

"Where's Top?" Jim demanded of Lee. The latter shook his head regretfully.

"They got him first crack, Uncle Jim. Top was trying to save our horses. As soon as it got dark I crawled over to where he lay. He'd been dead some time."

It had a shocking, galvanizing effect on all of them. Reb was the first to speak.

"Damn their dirty, rotten hides! They'll pay dear for this," he ripped out. "Neph and the other boys from Tumble L will be here directly. When they show up we'll give that bunch down there what they got comin' to 'em!"

According to Lee, he and his men had been attacked without warning.

"We fell back to the wagon at once and turned it over. The odds were not only four or five to one against us, but they had us out-gunned; we didn't have a rifle among us. As I told you, Top tried to get the broncs back out of range. They dropped him at once. They cut the wire then and got behind the herd. In no time at all they had the cows on the run. Half a dozen men — Duke Rucker was one of them — followed them up and closed in on us. We managed to turn them back. You know where that little swell rises below the road? Well, that's where they are. They've got their horses in there with them. We can't budge them from this direction. If you had smashed into them, as I thought you were going to do, they'd have cut you to ribbons!"

The experience had aged him, and he spoke with the authority of a seasoned man.

"We'll cut our fence and get around behind them, said Jim. "Bill, you go over to Pete. Tell him we're waiting for more men from Tumble L, that we'll go

214

through the fence as soon as they get here. You better stay over there. Move in a little when we go into action. We'll get them in between us if we can."

The better part of an hour passed before the men from Tumble L arrived. There were eight of them, since Neph had brought three of Lafoon's old crew along.

The fence had been cut, and the men waited impatiently for Brett to give the word that would send them streaming through. He had them gather around him first.

"I want you to listen carefully. I haven't any doubt we can move that bunch; their position offers no protection from the rear. When they break there's no telling which way they'll go. If they strike east, Pete and Bill will turn them back. What they'll most likely do will be to go through our gate and head south between here and the creek. It'll be a running fight. If necessary, we'll hang on to them all the way to Greely's Knob, and if that doesn't do it we won't stop this side of Ruby Lake. This fight isn't going to end in any draw! It's going to be settled for keeps!"

It was the feeling of every man who heard him speak. They left him in no doubt of that.

"But we can win this fight and still lose it if we leave this piece of range unguarded," Brett continued. "The stock that was run out of here will have to be driven back; the fence will have to be patched up. Otherwise, Curtis and his men will be in soon after daylight and Stash will have accomplished what he set out to do."

The men knew what was coming, and they shifted about uneasily, each hoping he wasn't to be kept out of the fight. Jim read their thoughts.

"I'm sorry," he said, "but some of you will have to stay behind. We'll all go in together, but as soon as we've got them on the run the men I'm going to name will have to drop out. In a long chase, I couldn't keep up with the rest of you, so I'll take charge here."

He named the men who were to remain with him. Tiny was one of them. The little man protested vigorously. "Top was my partner, Jim! You can't ask me to drop out of this ruckus till it's finished!"

"All right," Brett conceded. "I hadn't considered that. You Tumble L men, suppose you give us a hand with the cows. If you give a good account of yourselves, I'll see what I can do about jobs for you." He looked his men over. "I reckon we're all set. Let's go."

The advantage to be gained by engaging an enemy from the rear had been demonstrated on a thousand battlefields. To be successful, surprise was a necessary factor. That wasn't possible tonight. Stash had eyes. When he saw Brett's forces racing through the fence and disappearing on their wide swing to the west he knew what impended. He mounted his men at once, and a few minutes later they went through the fence too. They followed the road until they were within half a mile of Dutchman's Creek, and there they swung sharply to the south. Stash knew he was outnumbered now, but that was not the reason he failed to stand and give battle. By running he hoped to draw the enemy after him, thereby leaving the road unprotected; and he wanted it to be a stern chase.

Had he not been in such a hurry the maneuver might have been successful. But haste was its undoing. Topping a slight rise, Lee and Tiny glanced back and saw what was happening. Word was passed to Brett, and he immediately turned his force westward and reached the security of the creek bottom with minutes to spare. There, screened by the trees, they waited for Stash to appear.

"Hold off till they're abreast of us," Jim warned when they saw the foe coming. "Then let 'em have it."

Stash and his followers were taken completely by surprise. Grass Valley was upon them before they could whip out their guns. In that first savage attack Stash lost two men and had several others badly wounded. In danger of being surrounded, he knew flight was the only thing that remained to them; and it was urgent and imperative.

In the meantime Morrow and Pete, realizing that the fight had moved away from them and determined not to be kept out of it, had set out in hot pursuit.

Brett and the men who were to stay with him dropped out of the chase. Morrow and Pete flashed past them and joined it.

This wasn't the kind of pursuit Stash had wanted; it was too close, too punishing, and he couldn't shake it off. Into the lower Slate Hills it carried him. He attempted a brief stand there.

A slug carried Pete's hat away and gave him a bloody haircut. He tied a rag around his head and continued to pump his rifle. The other side paid a higher price: big Bill Dent's gun fell from his lifeless fingers as he rolled out of the saddle.

Greely's Knob was two miles away. At the head of his dwindling force, Stash raced for it. The Knob was just a wide place in the road, with a store and post office and several houses. Through it the fight roared. Directly in front of the post office Duke Rucker pitched to the ground.

"By cripes, that's one for me!" Lee heard Neph yell. A moment later Reb and Tiny drew abreast of them.

"Look out for that old stone corral up the road!" Reb shouted. "They may try to fort-up there!"

That had been in Stash's mind. He still had eleven men. Three, however, were in such shape that they couldn't fire a gun. "No," he decided at the last moment. "We'd be trapped there like a pack of rats."

To keep on running appeared infinitely more desirable. Gun belts were almost empty. He had five hundred 30-30 cartridges at Ruby Lake. If they could reach the house, they'd make their stand there.

His wounded couldn't hold the pace he set. When they fell behind he left them to shift for themselves.

The trail began to pitch upward to scrub timber and virgin pine as soon as they turned off the road. Once there had been good timber around the lake, but what remained was largely a tangle of worthless scrub. Some of Stash's men had only been waiting to reach it, ready to desert him at the first opportunity.

Four of them got away. Lee stopped a fifth. It left Stash with only four men able to give battle. Sixto

Guerra was one of them. When they flung themselves from their jaded ponies and rushed into the House, Grass Valley was pounding into the yard.

Guerra got Stash's ear. "The island out in the lake! You got a boat! Let's use it!"

"It won't hold five."

"It'll hold two," Guerra declared pointedly. "Give those three guys some cartridges and shove 'em out on the porch! We'll go through the back door to the boat!"

Sixto's beady, shoe-button eyes glittered in the darkness of the room. His words were an order; he wasn't merely advising Stash what to do. No longer was he the pliant tool who could be talked down to and dismissed with a few dollars for his services. The past three hours had stripped away all the pretense with which Stash had dressed the relationship between them. They were down to bedrock now.

"Yeh!" Stash gulped, knowing he didn't dare to disagree. He crossed the room and told the three men to get out on the porch and hold the Grass Valley men off as long as they could. When the wretches demurred, it was Guerra who changed their minds.

"Get out there before I drill you," he droned forbiddingly.

As Tiny said afterward, it was like shooting ducks on a pond. A few searching shots got the range. Slugs began to find the porch, then, splintering wood and smashing windows.

It was all over in the space of a few minutes; no one could remain on the porch and live. The three men reeled down the steps, the clothes literally shot off them, and raised their hands in surrender.

Lee believed Guerra and Stash were still in the house. Riding close, he leaped to the porch and ran in. He had to feel his way in the darkness. A step sounded behind him and swung him around. It was Neph Gibson.

"Git outa here!" Neph cried. "The house is afire! Yore brother and Guerra did a sneak out the back door!"

"Where are they now?" Lee demanded, refusing to budge until he had his answer.

"They're swimmin' out to the island! Reb and Tiny saw 'em and shot the hell outa of the tub they was in!"

The house, tinder-dry, began to burn fiercely. Lee and the rest stood watching it go. Pete suggested that they build a raft and get out to the island.

"No," Lee advised, "and I know I'm speaking for Jim as well as myself. We've got other plans for squaring accounts with that pair. Our job for this night is finished."

Surprising developments were to follow. The withdrawal of the surveyors and the abandonment of the new road was a relatively minor one as far as Lee and Brett were concerned. Stash and Guerra had appeared in town. Powder City, rocked, by news of the big fight, was buzzing afresh. Morgan Cameron had turned Stash adrift. Holderness, the Twin Buttes foreman, had been put in charge of the Cameron ranches temporarily.

"I don't see how we can hold back any longer, Uncle Jim," Lee felt compelled to say. "I wanted to get Kit away from Wyoming for two or three weeks as soon as I could. All this fighting and turmoil have been too much for her. But we'll have to wait. The thing for us to do is go to town and see the district attorney."

"When had you planned to get married?" Jim asked.

"We were going to drive into town Saturday evening, be married at the parsonage, and take the eleven o'clock train for California."

"Well, you go ahead; don't change your plans at all. I can handle this by myself and that'll make it a lot easier on you and Kit. I'll make it my business to be in town on Saturday. After you've taken the train I'll get together with Marsh and the prosecutor. If you young people can stand living here with me, I'll have this house fixed up spick-and-span and build a mess room down in the yard for the crew."

"I don't know of anything we'd like better," Lee assured him. "We had planned to move in with you as the place stands."

Brett shook his head. "No, it ain't fit for a woman of Kit's taste. You tell her I said she's to pick out the furniture and the fixings."

News of the wedding and the young couple's honeymoon plans was chronicled in the *Gazette*. Morg carried the paper to his office and locked the door. His world lay in ruins, but here was something of which he could be proud. He wanted to go to Lee and try to make amends. It was a step he knew he couldn't take.

Everything had gone wrong for him, even the road, which he had thought would put an end to conflict.

"I'd be misunderstood if I went to him," he muttered dismally. "Some day the boy may be moved to come to me; that's all I got to live for now."

He had not only dismissed Stash; he had thrown him out of the house and stripped him of everything. Stash was as dead to him as though he were in his grave.

Stony brought him word the following day that Lee was in town, making the arrangements with the minister and purchasing his tickets for California. Morg waited all day, hoping against hope that Lee would step into the bank and ask for him. He didn't come.

Thursday and Friday dragged by. When the bank closed at noon Saturday Morg was the last to leave. He had been taking his meals at the hotel, but today he walked home and had Stony get him a bite to eat. At the hotel he would have to talk to people, and he was not up to it.

The two of them sat down in the kitchen together. Stony had moved into the house at Morg's request.

"I saw Jim on the street this noon," Stony volunteered. Morg's long silences rested heavily on the old cowboy. "I asked him if there was anythin' to the talk that he's goin' to run against Hutton this fall. He says he won't permit his name to go before the convention."

Morg wasn't interested in politics. "Did he have anything to say about Lee?"

"He left him out at the station with the rig. They drove down from the ranch together, and Jim rode in alone. Lee's goin' to drive in this evenin' with the Mosbys."

Hope burned lower than ever in Morg. "I thought he might come to town this afternoon," he said woodenly. "It's just a short ride in from the station."

"A man's got plenty to keep him busy when he's gittin' married," Stony observed. "But he may come in, he might change his plans." This was strictly for Morgan's benefit.

All afternoon Morg sat on the porch, his eyes glued on the road. No one came, not even Stony. Twilight faded. Downtown the street lamps glowed feebly. Morg still sat there. At last someone came up the walk. It was Stony. His step was hurried, and when he ran up the porch there were unmistakable signs of excitement in him. He reached for the screen door and would have run up the stairs. Morg called him back.

"What's the idea?" he demanded. "What you after?"

"My gun," was the flinty answer. "I'm goin' to do what I shoulda done weeks ago. Stash is crazy drunk; he's been shootin' off his mouth that Lee ain't never goin' to marry Kit Mosby. He's gone out to the old icehouse to wait for him. He knows they'll have to pass within ten feet of the buildin'. I'm goin' out there as quick as a horse will carry me, and blow his head off!"

"No!" Morg cried in his agony. "No, you ain't, Stony! This job is up to me. I'll get my gun. You throw a saddle on a horse for me!"

"Morg, yuh ain't so quick on the trigger no more," Stony, protested. "Let me take care of this."

"Do as I tell you," was the level answer. For the moment, this was the old Morgan Cameron speaking.

Stony had done his bidding too long to demur now. Torn with anxiety, he saw Morg ride away. He stood it as long as he could, then hurriedly saddled up. As he dashed through town he saw Jim on the sidewalk. He pulled his bronc to a slithering stop and told him what was afoot.

"I've got a horse here," said Brett. "I'll go on with you. Stash will turn his gun on Morg as quick as he would on Lee!"

The old icehouse, long unused; had fallen to ruin. Jim and Stony found no signs of life there. If Morg and Stash were inside there was no sign of their horses.

"They coulda left 'em back in the brush," Stony ground out. "Have yore gun ready. I'll take one wall and yuh take the other. Don't shoot Morg by mistake. If yuh locate Stash, kill him on sight."

They slipped through the open door into the pitch darkness of the icehouse and parted without a word. Jim took a dozen steps and stopped short. Something loomed ahead of him. He listened, and caught the champing of a horse mouthing his bit. He reached the animal and ran his hand over the saddle. The tooling on the saddle skirt was familiar and he knew this was Stash's horse.

There was no sound from Stony; the sawdust on the floor permitted a man to move noiselessly. Suddenly the old place was alive with sound. First there was

Morg's growling: "You damned fool! I told you I'd handle this!" Hard on its heels came the crash of a gun. In the glow of the muzzle redness Jim saw Stash crouched down behind a beam. Stony saw him too. His .45 barked wickedly. Not only once. There wasn't retribution enough in that first shot for Old Stony, though it tore a ragged hole through Stash's heart. Standing over him, the old man emptied his gun into the lifeless carcass.

Jim took Morg's arm and led him outside, explaining how he came to be there. He had much more to say. By the time he had finished, Morgan Cameron knew what had impelled Lee's decision that night at Grass Valley. Guerra's attempt to kill Lee at the bank corner and the slaying of Ben Lafoon were recounted without mercy for Morg.

"I could have forgiven you everything if you hadn't tried to put that road over on us," said Brett.

"You're blaming me for the one decent thing I tried to do," Morg told him. "There'd been trouble at Edwards's gate. I knew there'd be more when you put up your fence. I thought the road would end all that. I wanted to be done with fighting. I never figured it would work out the way it did. You'll learn the truth some day, and you'll find it easier to believe than you do tonight."

Incredible as it was, Jim could not disregard it. "I'll withhold judgment," he said. "This is Lee's wedding night. We don't have to spoil it; we can hold back on what's happened here until he and Kit have left . . . I want to see them get married, Morg. Don't you want to be there too?"

"My God, yes, if I thought I'd be welcome!" There was no blasphemy in his heart. Unheeded, a tear ran down his cheek.

"Welcome? Of course you'll be. We'll walk in together. Nothing could make those youngsters so happy."